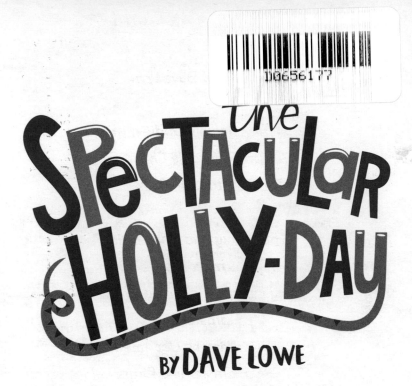

# THE SPECTACULAR HOLLY-DAY

### BY DAVE LOWE

**Illustrated by The Boy Fitz Hammond**

Piccadilly
PRESS

First published in Great Britain in 2017 by
PICCADILLY PRESS
80–81 Wimpole St, London W1G 9RE
www.piccadillypress.co.uk

A CIP catalogue record for this book is available from the British Library.

ISBN: 978-1-84812-611-4
*also available as an ebook*

1

Printed and bound by Clays Ltd, St Ives Plc

Piccadilly Press is an imprint of Bonnier Zaffre Ltd,
a Bonnier Publishing company
www.bonnierpublishing.com

*To Pippa – wishing you a lifetime of adventures.*

*And to Stace, Bec and Miri, as usual,
for putting up with my dad jokes. (Seriously
though – mushrooms **are** fun guys to be with.)*

# 1  The Envelope

I was lying in bed reading my atlas when Mum and Dad came in to see me – together.

I snapped the book shut and sat up.

Mum or Dad often came into my room at night to say goodnight or to tell me for the second or third or sometimes fourth time to stop reading and turn my light off. But whenever they came in together, it usually meant Something Big. And here they were, standing side by side, with funny looks on their faces.

My dad pretty much always looks funny – he was born that way, I guess. But Mum had this same strange expression too. Something was definitely up.

They'd both come to my room three years ago, to

break the news that my goldfish, Splashy, had died. Then there was the time that Granddad got sick and needed an operation – that was a Mum-and-Dad joint visit too, and so was the time they announced I was going to have a little brother. That was brilliant news of course, though what I hadn't realised at the time was how little peace and quiet there'd be in the house after Ernest was born, and just how much poo.

I squinted at Mum and Dad. My mind was whirring as I went through all the possibilities. Was I going to have another new brother or sister? I wasn't sure I could cope with *two* little people screaming their heads off the whole time, not to mention the extra pong.

Or, even worse – was one of my grandparents poorly? Or Mr Pike, our elderly neighbour? Or our dog, Oates?

Mum must have seen the growing panic in my eyes, because she smiled reassuringly and handed me an envelope which had my name on.

I took it as if it might be booby-trapped.

'Go on,' she said. 'Open it.'

I did. Slowly.

Then I gasped with excitement.

Inside was an aeroplane ticket! In my name! The destination: Malaysia!

'We're going together,' Dad announced. 'For five nights. Me and you. Just the two of us.'

I whooped, leapt out of bed, and hugged them both.

My dad's a travel writer – his actual job is to go round the world having exciting adventures. And I completely love exploring too, although my travels have only been local – until now!

I knew a bit about Malaysia from my atlas. It was hot, and there were jungles and orang-utans.

'We're going to the jungle!' I squealed.

Dad waggled his head. 'Well – not exactly, Holly. I've been invited by this fancy-pants hotel – The Ocean View – to write about it for the travel section of the weekend paper, and they've said I can take a guest.' He looked at Mum, then back at me. 'Mum's too busy. Ernest is too dribbly. And Oates is much too doggy. You're nearly eleven, and Mum and I both agree that you're grown-up enough to join me.'

Malaysia! On an actual Dadventure!

I couldn't wait to tell Mr Pike.


I've got friends my own age. I just want to point that out straight away. There's Asha and Jaya, the two Jacks and Harrison. But once a week I hang out with Mr Pike, who lives four doors up the road. He's seventy-six years old, and he teaches me magic.

Not 'magic' in a Harry Potter kind of way, of course. I mean, he can't do spells or defeat evil or fly on broomsticks – he can't even *walk* more than a few steps. He's got this electric wheelchair, which he drives like it's a getaway car. But he used to be a magician on stage, doing card tricks and rope tricks and sawing his glamorous assistant (Mrs Pike) in two.

Mrs Pike died a few years ago (but definitely not because of being cut in half by Mr Pike – she just got really poorly). So now he lives by himself and once a week I take him some home-made biscuits or a slice of cake, and he teaches me magic.

I used to be really frightened of him. He's got this scary reputation, but he's actually a real softy once you get to know him – like a sheep in wolf's clothing.

Three days before I was due to go on my Malaysian Dadventure, I was sitting in my usual armchair in Mr Pike's living room and he was in his wheelchair facing me, demonstrating a new trick – the disappearing coin. At least, the trick was new to me. Mr Pike performed it like he'd done it thousands of times before.

It went like this:

He put a shiny silver coin in his hand. Closed his hand. Opened it. No coin.

I actually gasped.

'But . . .'

He did the trick again. I watched super-carefully this time, without blinking, but the coin still vanished. And then – it was back.

I frowned and shook my head.

'How . . . ?' I said.

'Misdirection.'

'Is that like getting lost? Because my dad's really good at that.'

'No, what I mean is . . .'

His words trailed off, because something outside in the garden had caught his eye. I looked out of the window too but couldn't see anything unusual.

But when I looked back at Mr Pike, the silver coin was balanced in front of his left eye, like it was a monocle. He blinked it out into his hand and smiled.

'That,' he said, 'was misdirection. I got you to look the other way. But it can be done with real subtlety too. With just a slight movement of the hand, or a little glance, or a cough. Watch.'

He did the trick again, but in super-slow motion this time, and I finally saw how he did it: he glanced at his right hand and pretended to put the coin in there but it was his left that was now holding it.

'Wow – you make it look so easy.'

'It really is – after fifty-five years of practice. You're a pretty fast learner though, Holly. You'll be able to master it in fifty-three.'

I gave him a look.

'Ah – I'm just pulling your leg. After a few days of doing it in front of the mirror, you'll start to get the hang. Go on. Have a try.'

I did. My first five attempts were terrible. Even Oates wouldn't have been fooled. Then Mr Pike showed me again and this time he talked me through it, step by step. My next few tries were still clumsy, but better.

'That's today's homework,' he said. 'Practise it at home. Now, before you go, I've got a challenge for your Malaysian expedition.'

Mr Pike, back when he wasn't so old, visited loads and loads of countries – even more than Dad. He and Mrs Pike worked for years on cruise ships, travelling the world and doing magic shows as 'The Amazing Mysterio and The Enchanting Shakira' – which was definitely a more magical name than 'Mr and Mrs Pike'.

He knew all about my Dadventure – because he'd helped me with it – and I'd also told him – in great detail – about the Mumbelievable Challenge. So he knew my reputation for taking on difficult challenges.

'My task is for you to eat a durian,' he said.

'What's that? Some kind of bug?'

8

I pulled a face, because I knew that in some Asian countries, people actually do eat insects – crickets on skewers, for example, like they're chicken kebabs! I'd seen it on a travel show on the telly, and I wasn't at all keen on nibbling creepy-crawlies of any kind.

I'd accidentally swallowed a fly once, during sports day at school. It was near the end of the 400 metres. I'd been running with my mouth open and the fly had flown in. Obviously it didn't end well for the fly, but it wasn't brilliant for me either – I started choking, and spluttered to a stop in my lane, bent double. Emily Fellows had been watching and fell about in a fit of hysterics. Dad had been cheering me on but – after he'd made sure I was okay and fetched me some water – he helpfully suggested that I should swallow a spider to catch the fly, followed by a bird and then a cat and a dog and so on, like the old woman in the nursery rhyme. That was typical Dad.

The fly had been completely disgusting, and I never wanted to taste another insect in my life. But Mr Pike was grinning.

'A durian is most definitely not a bug,' he said. 'It's

this very large fruit – it's popular in Malaysia. And your task isn't to eat the whole thing, Holly. Just a mouthful will be enough.'

I frowned at him. The challenges I get from Mum and Dad are normally – well, really *challenging*. Was he seriously just asking me to try a tropical fruit? I *love* tropical fruit – mangoes, pineapples, lychees. But I shrugged, then smiled and said, 'Sure.'

# 2   Challenges

Mr Pike wasn't the only one to set me a challenge.

On the day before our trip, the final lesson was geography, and Ms Devenport put aside the last fifteen minutes to focus on Malaysia: she talked about the people, the culture and the wildlife, and then we watched a short video from the internet. It looked amazing – colourful and exciting. There was snorkelling, and orang-utans and monkeys and loads of delicious-looking food.

Everyone knew about my previous adventures, so she asked the class if anyone had a task that they would like me to attempt while I was over there. Before the lesson, she'd checked with me that this would be okay, and I'd nodded – but now I was blushing: a medium amount.

**BLUSHOMETER**

I still wasn't 100% comfortable being the centre of attention, but it was much nicer to be known as 'the kid who had exciting adventures' than 'the kid who does magic' or – worse – 'the kid whose dad wrote – *in a national newspaper* – about her nudie-run in a hotel'. Or 'the kid who got so scared on the class trip to the indoor rock-climbing centre that she got stuck halfway up the wall and had to be talked down by the instructor'.

'So,' said Ms Devenport, 'does anyone have any special Malaysian challenges for Holly?'

Harrison Duffy's hand shot up. His hand was pretty much always the first one to go up, but by the time the teacher called on him he'd usually forgotten whatever it was that he was going to say.

This time, though, he remembered.

'My challenge,' he said, grinning at me, 'is to bring a monkey back.'

Everyone laughed. Including me. Even Ms Devenport couldn't keep a straight face.

'I'm pretty sure that would be completely illegal, Harrison,' she said. 'Not to mention incredibly dangerous and – to be honest – not particularly nice for the poor monkey. How about we make Holly's challenge to *see* a monkey in the wild, rather than capture one and smuggle it home?'

Harrison nodded and so Ms Devenport wrote it up on the board. Lots of other hands were up by now – she looked around the room and chose Asha, my best friend.

'My mum says that people over there eat curries from banana leaves instead of plates, and use their bare hands instead of knives and forks . . .' Some of the class (especially Emily Fellows and the Harmer twins) made 'yuck' noises, but most other kids (including Harrison) thought that this sounded extremely cool. '*And* they eat fish-head curry,' Asha continued. This time, pretty much everyone said 'yuck' – even Harrison. I joined in too – I definitely wouldn't want to eat something that was staring right back at me.

Ms Devenport came to my rescue. 'How about we make the challenge "Eat five interesting local foods"?' she suggested. I nodded, relieved that fish head was off the menu.

She wrote this second task on the board and, while she was there, added another one of her own.

### 3. Write us a blog about your time there.

Ms Devenport was a regular reader of my dad's blog, called 'The Jimpossible Journey'. She thought he was completely hilarious. Dad thought the same thing too, so that made at least two of them.

'Any more tasks for Holly?' she said, looking around the class again.

Jack C's challenge was to learn some Malaysian words,

**14**

so Ms Devenport did an internet search and found that there were actually loads of languages over there, and that the main one was called 'Malay'. She wrote Jack's task on the board too.

### 4. Learn five new words or phrases to teach us when you get back.

Then she looked at her watch. There was only a minute to go before the bell.

'Let's have one more challenge for Holly,' she said.

A few people still had their hands up, including Emily Fellows, and I was silently begging Ms Devenport not to pick her, because she had this evil glint in her eye and was bound to choose something completely mean or something that could actually kill me. Or possibly both. *Please don't pick Emily*, I said under my breath. *Anyone but Emily.*

Ms Devenport said, 'Emily.'

I closed my eyes and prepared for the worst.

'I challenge Holly to climb something and not get stuck,' she said.

There were a few titters – from the Harmer twins especially, who even had identically horrible high-pitched laughs: they sounded like rats with their tails on fire.

Ms Devenport frowned, not understanding Emily's joke. 'Climbing is not really specific to Malaysia though, is it?'

Emily shrugged. 'How about running naked around the hotel then?'

There was more laughter, and Ms Devenport finally realised that I was being teased.

But even seeing the teacher's face and knowing that Emily was going to be told off didn't stop me from turning fire-engine red.

After school, things got even worse. Dad took me to get the injections I'd need.

'Apart from missing you guys,' he said, 'needles are the worst thing about being an explorer. With all the travelling I've done, I've been jabbed more times than a hedgehog-juggler.'

My injections stung – a bit. But after the doctor's, I soon cheered up. I finished packing and then wrote up the list of my challenges. Ignoring Emily Fellows's ones, but including Mr Pike's, there were five. I was ready.

# 3   Arrival

The flight was completely bottom-numbing and it seemed to go on forever.

Dad had flown loads of times, of course, and he was a complete expert. He took his shoes off straight away, pulled on some special socks and placed a horseshoe pillow around his neck. He flicked through the in-flight magazine, read a couple of articles and tutted at how bad the writing was. Then, after checking that I was okay, he put his eye mask on and was dozing even before take-off. He snored a bit, but thankfully it was mostly drowned out by the noise of the engines.

I watched three movies and ate loads of free food, including two little packets of peanuts which each took about ten minutes to open and about ten seconds to eat. I looked out of the window quite a lot, at the clouds and hills and rivers below. It was really spectacular.

But being in the same seat for hours on end didn't suit me at all. I got really fidgety, like the time we'd had history with Mr Sidebottom, the supply teacher. His name was the only funny thing about him and, even though he was so old he'd probably lived through most of history himself, the lesson was still incredibly boring. But at least it only lasted two hours. The flight was much, much longer.

When we landed in Malaysia, it was evening. Dad seemed quite refreshed, but I was completely exhausted. We got off the plane, waited in a queue for a while, grabbed our bags from the carousel and when we finally got through Customs there was a man waiting with a sign that said 'Tim Clambers'. My dad's first name is 'Jim' and our last name is 'Chambers', but it was close enough. Dad checked with him, and he *was* our driver, so we followed him out of the airport to his taxi.

The heat completely blasted us.

I had known it would be hot, but a temperature

written in a book doesn't prepare you. I'd never felt anything like it before. This heat felt like it was coming from a massive hairdrier. The smell was something new too – smoky and sour at the same time, a totally different smell to the streets back home.

Driving from the airport to our hotel, my tiredness completely slipped away. I was suddenly wide-eyed, alert.

The driver seemed to think we were in a car chase in a movie – he drove the taxi like Mr Pike drove his wheelchair. Then I watched the other cars and realised that everybody else was driving like that too. Everyone was beeping on their horns, swerving in and out of lanes or braking sharply: there were people on bikes who weren't wearing helmets. There were huge, noisy, dirty buses coughing out clouds of thick grey smoke, and there were cars of all shapes and colours and ages.

TIM CLAMBERS

In the lane next to us were four people on one motorbike – an entire family! The dad was steering, the mum was at the back and two boys were sandwiched in the middle. I tried to imagine how Mum would feel if that was us – she'd probably be having a complete heart attack.

One of the boys on the motorbike turned to stare at me. I stared back. Then he smiled and so did I.

It was brilliant. Everything was noisy, the lights were bright and the road signs were in a language I didn't understand. It didn't feel like we were in a different country so much as on a completely different planet.

But the hotel, when we got there, was pretty much the opposite of the world outside. It was shiny, quiet and neat, the temperature was cool and everyone was really polite. There were no loud noises or bright colours and absolutely no interesting smells.

We checked in at reception and then went up to our room on the fifteenth floor in a lift that was silent and super-fast.

Our room was seriously amazing: two queen-sized beds, side by side. I jumped onto mine: unlike my single bed at home, it didn't squeak at all. The pillows were huge and plumped-up like massive marshmallows – if you had a pillow fight with these, you could take someone's head off. And nestled on top of the pillow was something small and brown.

At home, I live with a misbehaving dog and a brother who is being potty-trained, so I've learned to be really suspicious of any little brown things that happen to be lying around. But this turned out to be a posh chocolate, wrapped up. Dad had one on his pillow too, and tossed it over to me.

I ate them both – completely delicious – then turned on the enormous telly, which was actually more like a cinema screen, and flicked through the channels. There were movie channels and kids' channels in English and loads of channels in languages I didn't understand.

When I went to check out the bathroom, I laughed out loud – there was a telly in there too! You could be having a bath or sitting on the toilet, and watching TV!

Dad was on the balcony looking out at the stars and the dark waves breaking onto the moonlit beach below us. It was really peaceful. And then it wasn't: a man's voice – deep – was suddenly blaring through a speaker. He was half singing, half wailing. It was strange, foreign – and really loud.

Dad saw the surprised look on my face.

'It's the call to prayer,' he explained. 'He's telling the Muslim people that it's time to pray.'

We listened for a bit, then went back inside and

closed the balcony door. I looked around the room again.

'Can we even afford this, Dad?'

'Nope,' he said, grinning. 'Not in a million years.' I frowned at him, so he added, 'Luckily we're not paying.'

'Who *is*? The newspaper?'

'No. The hotel invited us. For free.'

I frowned at him, baffled. 'But . . .'

'Imagine I write something nice about this hotel – in my blog and in the travel section of the weekend newspaper. Lots of people will hopefully read it, and some of them might decide to come here for a holiday, and that's how the hotel makes money.'

'But what if you write something not so nice?'

He shrugged.

'Most people don't,' he said. 'Think about it – if someone gives you a free cake, and then asks you how it was, you're not likely to pull a face and say it was completely disgusting, are you? Plus – this seems like a really nice place, doesn't it?'

I nodded.

'That's how these things work,' Dad explained. 'The hotel gets some publicity. The newspaper gets a story and pays me for it, and *we* both get a free holiday. So everyone's a winner. Especially us.'

He grinned, but this was all a bit disappointing. I'd always thought of my dad as a fearless explorer. He'd written about the daring expeditions that he'd been on – to deserts, jungles and hiking up mountains through heavy snow. But now he just seemed happy to be here – at a luxury hotel, relaxing. Had he always been like this? Or had he changed? Had my dad gone soft?

He must have mistaken the disappointment on my face for exhaustion, because he smiled at me and said, 'Go and hop in the shower, Lolly! After a long flight, you just can't beat a shower.'

He was actually right about that. It was the best shower I'd had in my entire life. The showerhead was the size of a dinner plate and the cubicle was the size of our entire bathroom at home! Then there were the towels – they were enormous, thick and soft like the towels that snuggle babies in TV adverts for fabric softeners. When I'd dried myself off, I put on my penguin PJs (don't ask) and flopped into bed. The pillow kind of swallowed me up – in a good way – and I fell asleep straight away.

In the morning, we went down to the breakfast buffet and a woman in a smart uniform showed us to a table. There was tinkly piano music and the smell of toast, sausages and coffee.

There were *five* different juices to choose from. I had the only one I'd never heard of – guava. It was reddy-orange, and really nice. It was a drink, so it didn't really count as an 'exotic food' for the challenge, but I still had plenty of time.

A lot of the food here was really familiar though:

cereal, toast, tomatoes, baked beans, hash browns, sausages and bacon.

Dad took me over to a man with a chef's hat who had four pans on the go.

'He's an Egg Man,' Dad explained. 'He cooks your eggs while you wait, just how you like them.'

*Egg Man!* I imagined a superhero whose special power was perfectly cooked eggs.

I asked for scrambled, Dad went for poached and, while we stood there watching him cook, I said to Dad, 'He's brilliant, isn't he?'

Dad nodded. 'He's a real eggs-pert.'

I sighed, but Dad wasn't about to stop.

'He's hilarious too,' he added. 'He knows loads of funny yolks. He's a real crack-up.'

I gave Dad a look.

When our eggs were ready, we took our plates back to a table and sat down. Dad's plate was stacked with fried food, with the poached eggs balanced precariously on top – and he seemed pretty impressed with the whole thing, until he cut into a sausage.

'Chicken sausages,' he said, tut-tutting. 'Muslim people don't eat pork. Which is fair enough. But a chicken has no business being anywhere near a sausage. And don't get me started on beef bacon.'

I didn't get him started on beef bacon. Instead I asked him whether we could go outside after breakfast – to explore. The hotel was really nice, but the taxi ride from the airport had got me craving more excitement.

'Look,' he said, 'we'll definitely explore – later on.

But our main job here is to experience everything the hotel has to offer first, so I can write about it. I've been scheduled for a spa treatment this morning. And I've booked you into something called "Adventure Club'", which – I have to say – sounds like much more fun than a spa.'

But he was wrong about that. Very wrong indeed.

# 4   Adventure Club!

It was the exclamation mark on the 'Adventure Club!' sign that had me worried. Whenever Ms Devenport uses exclamation marks on the board, it usually means that the lesson is going to be boring or tricky, or both.

For example: 'Maths Test!'

Or 'Reading Comprehension!!'

So I just didn't trust exclamation marks.

After breakfast, Dad led me to a brightly coloured room on the ground floor. One wall was yellow, one green, one blue, one orange. Nine or ten kids were already inside, almost all of them younger than me. There was only one boy who looked like he was my age, and he was sitting in the corner watching a movie on his iPad. There was a row of three games consoles along one wall, beanbags everywhere, a plastic table with loads of crayons for colouring-in, a craft table, a doll's house and a massive bucket of Lego.

My shoulders slumped. My suspicions had been right – this was basically a babysitting service for parents who wanted a few hours' break from their kids.

'Looks great,' said Dad as he signed me in. 'Lego! Beanbags! I wouldn't mind spending the morning here myself.'

I was about to ask him if he wanted to swap, when he gave me a hug, ruffled my hair (although I'm nearly *eleven*) and said goodbye.

A very bubbly woman with dark curly hair and a bright yellow T-shirt welcomed me with a high-five. It turned out that the helpers at Adventure Club – three young, super-energetic women – were very big fans of exclamation marks too.

'Hey, Holly!' the curly-haired one said: her name badge said 'Deb'.

'Welcome, welcome, welcome!' said a taller one with very long hair: Sara.

'Come join us!' said the third one – Tiggy, who was smaller and even smilier.

The three of them were possibly the most enthusiastic people I'd ever met. Dad sometimes gets a bit like that after a coffee – Mum calls him 'hyper' – but he usually calms down before long. The helpers all looked like they'd woken up this way – as if they'd bounced out of bed with huge smiles on their faces.

I was happy to go and sit in a corner and practise the disappearing coin trick all morning, but they wouldn't leave me alone until I'd done an activity, so I went to the Lego table and built a house. When I'd finished, Deb came over to tell me how completely awesome my house was, but it wasn't even slightly awesome. It was just a square box with a door and only one window, and the roof didn't quite join up – so if there was any rain in Legotown, the Lego family living there would be getting completely soaked. But Deb was gushing about how incredibly talented I was, as if I'd just built a scale model of the Taj Mahal.

Then there was a mask-making activity, which they cajoled everyone into doing – apart from the kid in the corner with the iPad. It was the same with the game of musical statues, later. The boy wasn't joining in at all, but the helpers just left him alone. They should have given him first prize though – he was actually the best statue of all. His eyes were the only part of him that seemed to move, as he stared transfixed at the movie on his iPad.

The three helpers were really nice people, but it was all pretty exhausting – I felt like I was trapped in a kids' TV show. After musical statues I really needed a rest, so I went over to the boy in the corner and sat next to him, figuring that they'd leave me alone too. He looked a bit lonely, and I used to be that way at school myself, so I knew how it felt. Maybe he really wanted to talk to someone but was just too shy.

He was watching a superhero movie, holding his iPad only a few centimetres from his face.

'Hi,' I said. He glanced at me, grunted and looked back at the screen. 'I'm Holly.' He grunted again, but this time didn't look away from the movie. Very slowly, I said, 'Do you speak English?'

'Yeah,' he said, like this was a ridiculous question.

'What's your name?'

He sighed and said, 'Patrick.'

'Are you from the USA?' I said excitedly, because he seemed to have an American accent and I'd never met an actual American before.

'Canada,' he said, as if I'd insulted him.

'How old are you?' I asked.

'Eleven.'

'Me too. Well, nearly. Is that a good movie?'

'Yeah.'

'Do you ever give more than one-word answers?'

'Nope,' he said.

'How's your holiday going?'

He sighed. A loud one. Then he paused the movie and actually looked at me.

'I'm not on holiday,' he said moodily. 'My dad runs a company and he's always busy, so I have to go away with Mum a lot of the time. She's a VP of this hotel chain.'

'VP?'

'Vice President. A big boss,' he said, explaining it to me like I was a little kid who didn't understand anything. 'She travels around, visiting hotels, checking up on things, and I get dragged along. To Singapore, Malaysia, Thailand, Vietnam.'

'Sounds great.'

'It's not. At every single hotel, I get thrown into Adventure Club. The staff are always this annoying –' he jerked his head towards the helpers – 'and the kids are even worse.' He glanced at me, pressed play on his movie, turned the sound up and completely ignored me.

I stood up, totally irritated.

'Nice talking to you too,' I muttered. Because sarcasm always makes me feel at least a tiny bit better.

When Dad came to pick me up, I was sitting by myself on a bright yellow beanbag, practising the disappearing coin trick, but really wishing that I could do the disappearing Pat-trick.

As soon as I saw Dad, I jumped up, made the coin disappear (into my pocket), thanked Deb, Sara and Tiggy (and got three high-fives from them – a high-fifteen), before leaving.

Dad was moving much more slowly than me, looking super-relaxed after his spa treatment.

As we walked back to the lift, he said, 'So how was Adventure Club? Give me the highlights.'

'Highlights? Let me see. I came fourth in musical statues. And I talked to the rudest kid in the entire world.'

'Ha,' he said. 'The women seemed really nice though.'

'Yeah,' I admitted. 'They were.'

I pressed the button and we waited for the lift. Dad had this huge idiotic grin on his face. I'd been planning to have a bit of a sulk about being put into Adventure

Club, but it was hard to be grumpy when Dad was in this kind of mood. His tactic was to wear you down with happiness.

'Ask me how the spa was,' he said.

I sighed. 'How was the spa?'

'Someone just massaged my face. My eyebrows! My ears! It was incredible!'

'And I built a small house from Lego,' I said, adding sarcastically, 'So we've both had brilliant mornings.'

He laughed, which made me smile – I couldn't help it.

When we got into the lift, I noticed a very strange sign.

'That's weird,' I said. 'No hedgehogs allowed?'

'It's not a hedgehog,' Dad said, cracking up. 'It's a durian. A kind of fruit.'

'Ah.' So this was the fruit that Mr Pike had challenged me to taste. I was suddenly a bit worried. 'Why are they banned from lifts? Do they explode or something?'

Dad giggled. 'Exploding fruit,' he said. 'You're hilarious. No, they're banned from lifts – and buses, actually – because they completely, absolutely stink.'

'Really?'

'Really. They pong – like they're rotting. They smell even worse than Oates's farts. I'm not kidding.'

Suddenly, Mr Pike's challenge didn't seem so easy after all.

We got changed into our swimmers and spent the afternoon down at the hotel pool. The water was warm and I was in there so long that my skin got all wrinkly, like Granddad's. Dad had a bit of a dip too, then smothered himself in suncream and lay on a sun-lounger, reading a book and occasionally jotting something down in his notepad.

He took his little notepad with him everywhere. Well,

not into the pool of course, but pretty much everywhere else. He was terrified of having a good idea and not being able to write it down. Mum explained to him that most people these days used their phones for that kind of thing, but Dad said it wasn't the same as pen and paper. So he took his notepad with him wherever he went. Mum said that he'd even scribbled down an idea during a wedding ceremony once – but thankfully, she'd added, it wasn't his own wedding.

I got out of the pool and stood over him, dripping. 'What's the plan for later?'

'We're supposed to sample the hotel buffet tonight,' he said. 'It's called the Seafood Spectacular.'

'Does it have an exclamation mark?'

'What?'

'The Seafood Spectacular.'

He shrugged. 'I think so.' Then he must have seen my reaction, because he squinted at me and said, 'I thought you liked seafood. And the word "spectacular".'

'I do.'

I really didn't want to seem spoilt and ungrateful – like Patrick from Adventure Club – and I knew that most kids would absolutely love it here: the pool, the buffets, the comfy beds, the best showers ever. I mean, *I* really liked it too. But the thing was – I'd been waiting my whole life for a foreign *adventure*. I'd spent hours in my room poring over my atlas, or spinning my globe – closing my eyes and stopping it with a finger to see where it would take me. Dad had told me plenty of stories about his own adventures, and I'd always imagined what it would be like to join him. I'd watched tons of wildlife documentaries and travel shows on TV and on the internet, and dreamed of visiting those places.

And here I finally was – somewhere foreign and exotic and exciting – but not able to have a proper look around. So I glanced down at Dad as he was sprawled on the sun-lounger. 'Someone once wrote that all posh hotels are pretty much the same.'

'Oh?' he said. 'Who was that?'

'You.' I remembered the quote word for word. '"Luxury hotels tell you hardly anything about the area where you're staying, or the culture, or the people."'

'Did I really say that?' said Dad, trying to keep a straight face. 'It doesn't sound like me.'

I rolled my eyes. 'Can't we go out, Dad? To explore? Please?'

He frowned. Then a big smile broke out.

'Of course we can,' he said.

# 5   Siti

It was five o'clock in the evening, but leaving the air-conditioned hotel for the street felt like stepping out of a fridge into an oven, and I started sweating straight away. It was still great to be out exploring though.

'Ah – sweet freedom,' I said, which made Dad shake his head and smile.

'You've been in a luxury hotel for less than a day, Holly. You're acting like you've been locked up in a maximum-security prison your entire life.' I laughed. 'So,' said Dad, 'where do you want to go?'

I looked up and down the busy street. There were people everywhere, taxis waiting, and these brilliant things that looked like huge tricycles.

Dad saw me staring at one. 'They're called trishaws,' he said. 'It's like a bike taxi. Shall we go for a ride?'

I nodded excitedly. There was one parked not far from us.

The driver was a grey-haired man wearing a white polo shirt and baggy shorts. He had bare feet, skinny legs and, when he smiled, I noticed that he had fewer teeth than Ernest.

'Where to?' he said.

Dad looked at me. I shrugged, so Dad turned back to the driver and said, 'Somewhere with no tourists, please.'

The driver frowned. 'But – you *are* tourists.' Then he smiled, said, 'Okay,' and we sat in the back.

I was worried that the man wouldn't have the strength to pedal us, because he was really bony and looked older than Granddad. But he turned out to be surprisingly strong – after a slow start, he really got up some speed, swerving around parked cars and tourists, and ringing his bell a lot, even when he didn't really need to, just for fun.

It was great. We were rattling around in the back – every bump in the road jiggled us – but that was all part of the excitement, and there was so much to see on the way: food stalls, little shops and people just milling around. A stray dog loped across the street. There were palm trees with strings of brightly coloured lights wound around them. There were people with menus trying to get tourists to eat in their restaurants, and men selling watches (fake ones, according to Dad). Best of all, there was a fruit stand, where a man with a huge knife –

actually, more of a cutlass – was expertly slicing up a pineapple that was balanced *in his free hand*! It was a complete miracle that he still had all his fingers. At least I think he did.

The further we went, the fewer people were around, the fewer things to see, and the bumpier and dustier the road. And then, after ten minutes, the driver stopped with a squeal of brakes, turned around to look at us, shrugged and said, 'Here?' as if he thought we were a bit nuts for wanting to come to a place like this.

'Lovely,' said Dad. 'Thanks.'

We got out and Dad paid him.

'You want I come back?' the driver asked.

'No – we're fine, thanks,' Dad said.

The driver shrugged, turned the trishaw around and pedalled off, ringing his bell as he went.

'Now what?' I asked.

'What I usually do in new places is just have a wander around and see what I find. But this time . . . *you* lead the way, Holly.'

We walked down the narrow street – houses were crammed together on both sides, and it looked like the people had built the houses themselves, out of whatever bricks and blocks and pieces of wood had been lying around. Some of the houses were nice, with colourful plants in pots outside, but some of them reminded me of my Lego house, except with more windows and – I hoped – roofs that went the whole way across.

When I walk up our street at home to visit Mr Pike, everything is usually quiet and calm, apart from an occasional car, or Emily Fellows having a complete tantrum. But here, kids were playing in the street, a man could be heard singing and a woman was laughing – the kind of laugh where I imagined her whole body would be shaking. There was the sizzle of frying food from another house. Birds warbling in the trees. Buzzing insects. A dog barking. Chickens clucking.

And the smells too! Frying chilli and garlic, burning incense, sewers, lemony cleaning fluid, flowers.

In front of us, a chicken crossed the road as if she owned the whole place. Dad whispered, 'Watch, and we'll find out the answer to the joke.'

The chicken took its time, pecking now and again, before wandering off.

'I guess it *was* just to get to the other side,' Dad said, looking very pleased with himself.

We kept on walking. I took a left and then a right, just following my instinct, and Dad followed me. He had a terrible sense of direction and I was beginning to think we should have left a trail of breadcrumbs so that we could find our way back to the hotel and get something to eat, but then we turned a corner and saw – well, you couldn't call it a restaurant, exactly. It was basically a metal cart by the side of the road, with a gas bottle. A small man was behind the cart, banging a wok around, cooking.

There were six plastic tables, each with four plastic chairs. Five of the tables were empty, and three local men were sitting at the other, wearing T-shirts and sarongs. A short waitress wearing a silky green dress was delivering drinks to them.

'You hungry?' Dad asked me. 'Thirsty?'

I was. Dad went up to the chef and tried to order something in an embarrassing combination of English, Malay and mime. The chef looked up from his wok and shook his head to show that he had no idea what on earth Dad was saying – and called the waitress over.

Then I noticed something really surprising: she was really young – about my age! She had shiny black hair in a bob, and a very nice smile.

'Can I help you?' she said.

Dad smiled back, relieved, and ordered some food and drinks in English. He paid, said a word in her language and then we went to an empty table and sat down.

'What was that you just said?' I asked him.

'I said "thanks". Wherever I travel, I always learn "hello", "thank you" and "sorry" – the three most important words in any language.'

I didn't ask Dad to teach me any of those, because it would have felt like cheating. I wanted to get my five words from actual Malaysian people, not from my not-at-all Malaysian dad.

The girl came over with a tall plastic cup of milky iced tea for Dad and a same-sized cup of chocolate milk for me. She smiled shyly as she placed our drinks on the table, and I wondered if she was working there as a part-time job, or if she was related to the chef. Did kids over here have to work? I wanted to ask her, but she might think I was being rude and, besides, my attempt at talking to Patrick earlier had gone incredibly badly, so maybe it was best if I stayed quiet.

I'd been hot and sticky and thirsty, but this drink was amazing – cold and chocolatey, with about ten ice cubes that rattled as I stirred it with the straw.

Not long after, the girl came back with our meals and Dad and I stared down at the plates of steaming food in front of us.

Two big orange plastic plates each had a huge mound of fried rice, with a fried egg balanced on top. I lifted the egg with a fork, like I was checking under a rug for something hidden. There was nothing underneath it, except more rice. But there were hunks of fried chicken on the side, slices of cucumber, some peanuts and some unidentified brown crispy things, smaller than my little finger.

This was definitely exotic enough for Asha's challenge, so I could tick one food off already – four to go.

I tried a forkful of the rice. It was tangy, hot and completely delicious. I had another forkful and another. It was a bit spicy, but not blow-my-head-off, and my drink did a great job of cooling down my tingling tongue.

It was all brilliant – except for the brown crispy things. They turned out to be tiny dried fish. I'm serious. Shrivelled, crispy little fishes. I pinched one between a finger and thumb, popped it into my mouth and crunched. It was really, really salty and – not surprisingly – very fishy indeed.

Ugh!

I spat it out into a tissue. Dad giggled, scooped the rest of the fishes from my plate and crunched them one after another, like they were crisps. He was having the best time, making 'mmm' noises, slurping on his tea and muttering, 'Great idea to come here, Holly. Genius. Best. Food. Ever.'

I grinned, and when we'd finished the girl came over to take our plates.

'It was okay?' she said.

'Okay?' said Dad. 'It was fantastic!'

I nodded enthusiastically and the girl smiled.

Dad ordered two more drinks and, when the girl brought them over and put them onto the table, she stood there very awkwardly for a few seconds. I was starting to worry that we'd done something wrong. Maybe spitting dried fish into a tissue was the worst possible insult in this country! But then she said, 'Excuse me. I am very sorry to bother you. But my teacher – my English teacher – she say to us, find a tourist, talk to him or her, write about them. We don't get much tourists around here. So – can I talk to you? It is okay?'

'Sure,' I said – and I was so happy that she was talking to me I wasn't even bothered that she'd called us tourists.

Dad stood up, saying, 'I'll leave you to it. I need to have a post-dinner stroll anyway, to walk off this delicious food.' Then he patted his tummy, and the girl giggled, embarrassed, which was a perfectly normal reaction to anything that my dad said or did.

Dad took his phone out and walked around, looking for random things to take photos of. A chicken. A wall. Meanwhile, the girl reached into the pouch where she kept the money for the restaurant, and pulled out a pen and the little notepad she used for taking the orders. Then she stood shyly in front of me until I asked her to sit down.

'What is your name?' she asked.

'Holly.'

'Holly. Like "holiday"?'

'No. Yes. A bit. H-O-L-L-Y.'

She wrote it down in her book. I smiled – so there was still someone in the world other than Dad who took notes in this way!

'And where are you from?'

I told her and spelled out the name of my town – she wrote that down too, and then asked me how old I was.

'Ten. Nearly eleven. And you?'

'Eleven.'

'What's your name?'

'My name is Siti. S-I-T-I.'

'How long have you been learning English? You're really good.'

'I started four years ago,' she said. 'The pencil is on the table.'

I looked on the table but there was no pencil, and so I frowned, confused, which made her smile – a big one that the whole of her face joined in with.

'We learned it at school,' she said. 'The first lesson was –"The pencil is on the table". "The pen is by the book".'

'Ah,' I said. 'We learn all that stuff in French too, but it's not so useful in real life, is it? Unless I go to Paris, I suppose, and get a job in a stationer's.'

I was expecting her to smile, but she gave me a blank look and I realised that I'd been talking too quickly – gabbling, probably – and she hadn't understood. Plus, 'stationer's' would probably be a tricky word for someone who was learning English. So I slowed down and said,

'Your English is much better than my French.'

'Thank you.'

'Is that your dad? The chef?'

'Yes,' she said. 'And that is your father?'

'Yes,' I sighed, because he was crouching and taking a photo of a flower that was growing through a crack in the concrete. Yet again, I'd won the battle of the embarrassing dads.

'Where is your mother?' asked Siti. 'And your siblings?'

'At home, in my country. I've got one brother. He's only two.'

'You are on holiday, only you and your father?' she asked, and looked at me like this was really strange. I suppose it was, a bit.

'He's working,' I explained. 'My dad. He's a writer.'

'A waiter?'

I smiled. Dad was forgetful and clumsy – he'd make a really terrible waiter. 'He's a *writer*. A journalist. For a newspaper.' I mimed writing and she nodded that she understood. 'Do *you* have brothers and sisters?' I asked.

'Oh, yes. Four brothers. Two sisters.'

'Wow!' I said, because I knew how much trouble just one brother could make. Four of them and two sisters?!

'Our house is sometimes like a zoo,' she said.

I laughed. 'Our house *smells* like a zoo sometimes. Because of my baby brother, and the dog.'

'You have pets?' she said, wide-eyed.

'Just a dog. I had a goldfish, but it died.'

She scribbled that into her notepad.

'Do you have any pets?' I asked.

She shook her head sadly. 'I would really like a cat.'

'Where do you live?' I asked. She pointed down the street, but there was a strange smile on her face. 'What?'

'My homework,' she said, her eyes twinkling, 'is to ask *you* questions, remember.'

We both laughed. She had a great laugh – soft and musical, the exact opposite of the Harmer twins'. She'd seemed really shy to begin with, but now I could see that she wasn't shy at all – she was confident and funny.

'Where do *you* stay?' she asked. 'Which hotel?'

'The Ocean View.'

Her eyes widened, as if I'd told her that I was living in a palace.

'It's great, yes?'

I shrugged. 'Yeah. It's okay.'

'"Okay"?' she said. 'It's fantastic. My older sister Nur works there as a cleaner. She says there are televisions in the bathroom! Also a big bath, enough for three people! But I'm not sure why you'd want a bath with three people.'

We both laughed about this, and I said, 'It *is* a really nice place,' because I didn't want to seem completely spoilt.

'But?'

'I just wanted something more – real – I suppose.'

She found this funny.

'What do you mean, "real"?'

'Like, normal. Like – the real Malaysia.'

Siti looked around at the small houses and the uneven street.

'Like, this real?' she said. I nodded. 'I think – this real is not so nice, comparing to the Ocean View Hotel.'

I shifted uncomfortably in my seat. I felt a bit like Patrick from Adventure Club – rude and ungrateful. So I tried to explain. 'All I mean is – I just wanted an adventure.'

She seemed to understand. A huge smile spread across her face.

'You can come tomorrow if you want,' she said. 'I'm here. No school!'

After a long, sweaty walk home, the air-con in our hotel was completely delicious. Back in our room, we called Mum. Dad spoke first, and then he passed the phone to me and went for a long shower.

'Hi, Mum.'

'Hi, Sausage. How are you? Dad said the hotel's great. And that you had amazing food tonight.'

'Yeah. Apart from the shrunken fishes. Yuck. You should have seen them.' Mum laughed. 'And I met this girl called Siti.'

'Great.'

'She's my age – well, a tiny bit older – and she's really funny and really nice. She works as a waitress in her dad's restaurant and we talked for ages until more people came and she had to work – she likes rock music and action movies, she's a Muslim but she doesn't wear a headscarf, she's super-smart and really friendly and she's got six brothers and sisters.'

'Wow,' said Mum, and I wasn't sure if she was reacting to the thought of having seven kids, or if it was because I'd explained all that stuff about Siti in ten seconds flat.

'She must speak really good English,' Mum said. 'Unless you've picked up the language really fast!'

'I think she understood most of what I was saying, and I got about ninety per cent of what she said too.'

'That's a higher percentage than when me and your

dad have a chat,' Mum joked. 'So, what's the plan for tomorrow?'

'Dad's got to go on a guided tour and then visit this place where they're going to build a hotel. But there's only enough room for the journalists, not for family members. So I've got to go to Adventure Club again. Woo hoo! That "woo hoo" was sarcastic, by the way.'

'I gathered that,' said Mum. 'But you know, Holly, if adventures don't find you, you sometimes have to go and make them happen.'

# 6   Adventure!

'Wake up, Holly!'

I opened my eyes and groaned. So would you, if the very first thing you saw in the morning was Dad's face staring at you, extremely close up – only ten centimetres away, in fact. I could see nostril hairs. Dad was leaning over me, shaking me gently by the shoulder and saying, 'We've both slept in! I've got to be in the lobby in four –' he glanced at the clock – 'three minutes! That's the problem with really comfy beds. I'll be back here at one o'clock. I'm really sorry, Holly – this is the last time we'll be split up this holiday. Promise. Now, can you get yourself to breakfast and Adventure Club?'

I grunted yes.

He staggered around the room putting his shorts on, then pulled on a T-shirt – first trying to fit his head through an arm-hole and then back to front, before eventually getting it right. He checked the clock again, and then leaned over and planted a kiss on my head.

'Gotta go,' he panted. 'Sorry – love ya!'

Dad was right about the bed – it was so comfy that I went straight back to sleep. It was super-quiet here too – just the hum of the air-con, which was a much nicer sound to wake up to than Ernest screaming his tiny head off, or Oates whimpering because he needed to be let outside for yet another wee.

When I woke up again, I sat up in bed watching *SpongeBob Squarepants* in a foreign language – some kind of Chinese, I think, though I couldn't be sure. Then I got dressed, stuffed my great-grandma's pocket watch, some money and the room key into my shorts pocket and went down in the lift. In the restaurant, the Egg Man had gone and they were clearing up after breakfast: I'd missed it. I checked my watch – half past ten.

I knew that if I went to Adventure Club right away,

I'd have at least two and a half hours before Dad came for me, and I'd be completely starving by then. They had apples there and bottles of water, but that was hardly a proper breakfast.

So I went to the lobby and stepped outside into the heat. I had a plan. I'd go to the nearest food place, eat something and then go straight back to Adventure Club. I was pretty sure that Dad wouldn't mind, and I would have had a little adventure, all by myself.

'Hello! Where to?'

I looked up. The trishaw driver from yesterday was there, in his seat. He rang his bell.

'You want go same place?' he said. 'Like yesterday?'

My mouth answered before my brain could catch up.

'Yes, please,' I said, and hopped in.

He pedalled off and – almost immediately – I felt bad: my chest tightened and my tummy was light. What was I thinking? There was a really good reason why I hadn't asked for permission to visit Siti today, why I hadn't even mentioned her invitation – because Dad would have said no. He was the one who always encouraged me to have adventures, but even he wouldn't have let me go exploring by myself in a foreign country. No way.

But then I tried to convince myself that this was really no big deal – I'd just be getting breakfast, saying hello to Siti, chatting for a few minutes and then coming straight back to the hotel. Dad had abandoned me, pretty much, and Mum had actually encouraged me to go looking for adventures.

I told myself all this but at the same time I knew that both Mum and Dad would go absolutely bananas if they found out what I was doing.

The trishaw ride last night had been brilliant, but now the same bumpy journey was making my stomach churn.

What if I didn't have enough money to pay the driver? I couldn't remember how much Dad had paid yesterday. And then what if I couldn't find Siti's house? What if she wasn't home? What if I couldn't find my way back to the hotel?

I completely wished I was in Adventure Club – hungry and bored, maybe, and almost certainly working out ways that I could annoy Patrick. But at least I'd be safe there, and out of trouble.

The man parked his trishaw in exactly the same place as yesterday and said, 'Okay?'

I nodded, but I was feeling sick. I took money out of my pocket and held it out to him – he took just a couple of coins from my palm, which was definitely less than Dad had paid last night.

'Special price,' he said. 'You want me wait?'

I was too embarrassed to say yes. Besides, what would I do while he waited? Look for Siti and then come back? I shook my head, so he turned the trishaw around, rang his bell, waved and pedalled off.

And then I was completely alone.

I took a deep breath and walked up the street, trying to remember the way we'd gone to Siti's dad's restaurant. My pocket watch has got a little compass, but that was no help to me now. Had we taken a left and then a right last night? Or was it the other way around?

A big woman in a bright purple dress and headscarf came out of her house with a bucket of soapy water and

emptied it onto her front yard, a little concrete area. I had to step into the street so my trainers didn't get splashed. When she saw me, she gave me a funny look.

'Siti?' I said. 'I'm looking for a girl called Siti.'

The woman frowned – not understanding – then she shook her head and went inside, and I felt queasier than ever.

When I eventually found the place where we'd eaten last night, I felt even worse. I'd been hoping that Siti would be there and that her dad's restaurant would be open for breakfast, so I could have a cold drink, a chat and something to eat. But it was completely empty. The chairs and tables were neatly stacked, upside down, and the cart where Siti's dad had cooked the food was covered in a blue waterproof sheet. There was no one around, not even any chickens.

I remembered the direction that Siti had pointed in when I'd asked where she lived, so I went that way and soon saw two boys – both around seven – playing in the street with a remote-controlled car. They stopped and stared at me as if I was some kind of alien.

'Hello,' I said.

'Hello-how-are-you-I'm-fine-and-you,' one boy said, and the other boy giggled.

'One-two-three-four-five,' said the second boy, and both of them laughed.

'I'm looking for Siti.'

They looked at each other and shrugged – they didn't understand what I was saying.

A tall, thin older man came out of one of the houses, wearing trousers, a vest and glasses, and when he noticed me he had a puzzled expression.

'Do you speak English?' I asked and – to my complete relief – he said he did. 'I'm looking for a girl called Siti. She lives near here.'

'Many girls here are called Siti.'

'She works with her dad,' I said, pointing to the food cart in the distance.

'Ah,' he said. He walked a few steps down the street, then shouted Siti's name and a few more words that I didn't understand.

We waited. The boys too.

Then Siti burst out of her house. At first she looked shocked to see me, and my heart sank – what if she'd only asked me to come here out of politeness, not thinking that I would actually do it? Or what if I'd misunderstood what she'd said – what if she hadn't invited me at all?

But as she walked towards me, a huge smile spread across her face, and I immediately felt much better.

'Hello,' she said. 'Holly-Holiday!'

'Hello-how-are-you-I'm-fine-and-you,' the first boy said, but Siti glared at him and the two boys went off to play with their remote-controlled car. The man in the vest went back into his house, which left just the two of us standing in the middle of the street, looking at each other and trying to work out what to say next.

# 7   Bananas

'So – what do you want to do?' Siti asked.

Actually, I wanted to go right back to the hotel. My tummy was still churning – I'd had enough adventure already just getting here, and I couldn't risk being late for Dad. But I also knew that I couldn't just turn up like this and then leave straight away – she'd think I was a complete weirdo. Plus, I still had more than two hours before Dad would be back, and part of me did want to do something exciting. This might be my one chance. So, when she asked me what I wanted to do, I said, 'It's up to you.'

'Up?' she said, frowning and pointing to the sky. I smiled.

'"It's up to you" – it means, like "it's your decision".'

'Ah,' she said. Then she repeated the phrase.

I had an idea.

'Are there any monkeys around here?'

She smiled and nodded. 'Some.'

'Can we go to see them?

'We can try,' she said. 'But they are sometimes –' she searched for the word – '*shy*. They live in trees near the beach.'

I followed her the short distance to her house. It was a small bungalow, but made of big blocks instead of bricks. In their small concrete front yard was a bench, a pot plant and a motorbike. Siti didn't go inside – just pushed the door open, poked her head in and shouted something. A woman's voice answered. And then we walked off, down the dusty street, further away from my hotel.

'Was that your mum? In the house.'

'Yes.'

'What did you say to her?'

'That I am going out with a friend, and I will be back later.'

That word – 'friend' – made me tingle.

'And what did your mum say?'

'She said okay.'

'Wow.'

It seemed like Siti could do whatever she wanted. Since my Dadventure I'd had a bit more freedom, but still nothing like as much as Siti. If I'd asked my mum for permission to go further than the end of our street, even for a few minutes, she'd definitely be asking me where I was going, who with, why, and for how long – and even then she might not let me go.

'You're so lucky,' I said.

Siti looked at me with this amused frown.

'*Me*, lucky?' she said, and then a huge grin broke out. 'You stay at The Ocean View.'

'Where I'm from, kids aren't usually let out of their parents' sight. We can't do anything without our mums and dads. You're free! You can do what you want, without your parents around.'

'Yes, but – if I make something wrong, they can hear about it in five minutes. Nawawi – the man who called me out from my home before – he will see my father

**73**

later and say, "I saw Siti with a foreign girl today" –' she did a really good impression of the man – 'and he will ask about it, and then the whole street will know. And also – yes, this morning I am free, but I usually have to go to school . . .'

'Me too.'

'. . . and I'm having more than one hour homework each night.'

'Every night?' I said. I have less than an hour's homework a *week*. Ms Devenport is really nice like that.

'. . . and I also have extra classes after school, four times each week,' said Siti. 'English on Monday and Wednesday. Science on Tuesday. Mathematics on Thursday. We go to mosque on Friday, and I work for my father some nights.'

'Wow,' I said, because that did sound like a whole lot. 'Why do you need extra classes for English? You're really good at it.'

'Thank you. But I am good because of the extra classes, I think. But they are *very* expensive for my parents. So I must work hard. To get a good job. Doctor. Engineer. Lawyer. Accountant.'

I didn't know any kids who wanted to be those things. Footballers or dancers, yes. Last week, Harrison wanted to be a spaceman. But accountants, no: not even Toby Brown, who was so quick at maths that Ms Devenport called him The Human Calculator. No kid in history had ever wanted to be an accountant.

I saw, for just a tiny moment, that Siti's smile had slipped. Mum always noticed things like that – she could spot a slightly sad expression from twenty metres away, and a guilty look from the other side of a room. It was like a superpower, and maybe some of it had been passed down to me.

'What job would *you* like to do though?' I asked.

She went quiet, and then said, 'Sometimes – not often – I get up very early in the morning and go to the beach to watch the crabs. Birds. Lizards. I think a job with animals would be nice.'

'So do *that* then.'

She shook her head – a tiny bit. And then she forced a smile, like she didn't want to talk about it any more. 'What about you, Holly?'

I shrugged. I'd always wanted to be an explorer like

my dad, but right now I wasn't so sure. Dad's job didn't seem like it was full of the death-defying excitement that I'd been imagining all those years. The only danger he seemed to be facing these days was from those enormous fried breakfasts.

We walked in silence for a while, until Siti said, 'Bananas.'

I gave her a funny look, because it was a very odd word to say, completely out of the blue like that. She laughed at my reaction, which made me burst out laughing too.

'It's my favourite word in English,' she said. 'Bananas, bananas, bananas. Would you like some? Are you hungry? Because I know a place.'

I nodded – I was completely starving.

I wondered if she was going to take me to a fruit shop, or to a man hacking bananas with a cutlass like the pineapple guy yesterday, or if we'd be climbing a tree to pick a bunch (I really hoped not – I was still pretty afraid of heights after the whole rock-climbing incident). But she didn't take me to a shop *or* a cutlass-wielding fruit-slicing guy *or* a tree: instead, we went to a man with a pan.

The man was wearing sandals, trousers and a white T-shirt – and was standing next to a little trolley which had a pot of hot oil, a bowl and a small gas bottle underneath. Next to the trolley were two big buckets. The man smiled when he saw Siti – he seemed to know her.

She said something, and he took a bunch of tiny bananas from the bucket, quickly peeled them one by one, dropped the peel in the other bucket, dipped the bananas in batter and then dropped them into the pot of bubbling brown oil. The whole operation took about twenty seconds, tops. His actions were super-skilful, like the Egg Man or like Mr Pike doing the coin trick.

As each little banana hit the hot oil, it made a really satisfying plop sound, and then a sizzle. I listened to Siti and the man as they talked and I breathed in the thick banana-ey smell and completely forgot about everything else: Dad, the hotel, Adventure Club. Everything. This was what I'd come here for. This was the experience I'd dreamed of my entire life.

I'd had adventures before, great ones – the original Dadventure and the wilderness challenge that Mum had dreamed up. But this – going out by myself in a new country, making a friend, buying deep-fried bananas (exotic food number two!) – this was the most exciting one yet. And it was a proper adventure too – one that was just for me, one that hadn't been organised by grown-ups.

After a minute or two, the man fished the bananas out of the oil with this scoop that looked like a big flat sieve and tipped them into a thick brown-paper bag, which he handed to me with a flourish like he was presenting me with a rose. I smiled and held out a palmful of coins. He took three and I worked out the cost in my head. The bananas were really cheap.

I asked Siti for the word for 'thank you'.

'*Terima kasih*,' she said.

So I thanked the banana man in his language and they both smiled, probably because of my terrible pronunciation. But still – it was my first new phrase.

We kept on walking.

I checked the time on my pocket watch. It was only eleven, so I still had two hours before I needed to be back at the hotel. I had the feeling that this adventure wasn't finished yet, not at all. There were hot bananas to eat, a beach to discover, and monkeys to find.

# 8 Monkeying Around

I shared the bananas with Siti.

She didn't take one at first but I was really persistent, and it turned out that she was just being polite – she was a really big fan of fried bananas. Who wouldn't be? They were golden and crunchy on the outside, warm sweet and gooey in the middle, and one of the best things I'd ever eaten.

After ten minutes we'd polished them off and arrived at the beach full and happy. Then – on the sand – she took her shoes off and walked barefoot towards the sea. I copied her, but that was a big mistake.

Her feet must have been used to the scorching heat of the sand, but mine definitely weren't. It was like walking

on hot coals. I yelped and hopped from foot to burning foot towards the water, making lots of 'ooh, ooh' noises, probably sounding like a monkey myself, and not a happy monkey either. Siti found this very entertaining.

The sea, when I finally reached it, cooled the soles of my feet straight away – like when you put a hot pan into a sink of cold water.

'Ahhh!' I said, which was maybe the loudest sigh of relief in history, and which made Siti laugh some more. So I splashed her. More laughter, from both of us this time, and we splashed around in the ankle-high waves for a minute or two, before she pointed out a smallish island towards the horizon. It looked spectacular – covered in trees, with a small beach of white sand. Like an island from a movie.

'There are *many* monkeys over there,' she said. 'Hundreds. We call that place "Monkey Island". There are many other animals there too – some people say there are even mouse deer living there.'

'Mouse deer?'

'It's a deer, but *this* big.' She showed me – it was the size of a hand.

I wondered if she was pulling my leg, but she looked completely serious.

'My uncle has taken us there in his boat, many times. But we cannot go there now, because it is private. Soon there will be a big hotel and most of the trees will be – how do you say it?' She made a chopping motion with her hand.

'Chopped down?' I said.

'Yes – and the monkeys will be gone too.'

'Gone? Where to?'

She sighed. 'They will put them in zoos, I think.'

I looked at the island and wondered if that was where Dad was right now.

Siti pointed to a cluster of trees a long way down the beach from us. 'There are not so many monkeys around here, but there are some.' We stepped out of the shallow surf, put our shoes back on, and walked down the beach.

'So, you like monkeys?' she said.

I shrugged. 'Not really.'

She looked at me like I was a complete weirdo, and I couldn't blame her: I'd asked her to take me to see monkeys, and then it turned out that I didn't particularly like them. So I tried to explain. 'Harrison challenged me to see one.' This seemed to confuse her even more.

'What is a Harrison? What is a challenge?'

I smiled. Describing a Harrison would be very difficult, so I just said, 'He's a friend of mine. And a challenge is like homework, kind of, but for my holiday. Some people gave me challenges to do while I'm here.'

This baffled her completely, so I told her about my other big adventures – which was really hard to do in simple English, but eventually she seemed to understand, and had this huge smile.

'My English homework is going to be the best ever,' she said. 'My classmates will probably just speak to someone for one minute – learn their name and age and country. I have your whole life story, Holly.'

My face felt hot, and not just from the sun.

'No,' she said, 'it's great. Thank you, Holly. *Terima kasih!* I am very happy!'

'What about *your* life story?' I asked.

She shrugged. 'It's boring.'

'You live *here*,' I said, looking at the beach and the sea and the blue sky. 'How can it be boring?'

'I don't live here though – on the beach. I live in a room with my older sister, who is sixteen and mostly angry.'

'You must have friends though.'

'Some. But I spend more time with my textbooks than with my friends. And my friends, too, are busy. My best friend, Damia, works in her family's shop. And studies a lot also. So I don't spend much time with friends, outside of school.'

'Except today,' I pointed out, and this made her smile.

'Except today,' she agreed.

As we walked towards the trees, she said, 'So, one of your challenges is to see a monkey?'

'Yes.'

'And what are the others?'

I told her about the blog and the two tasks that she'd actually already helped me with – the exotic food one and the language one.

She smiled and said, '*Bagus*.'

'Excuse me?'

'*Bagus*. Another word for your challenge. It means "good".'

'*Bagus*.' It was a really fun word to say – maybe even more fun than banana. '*Bagus, bagus, bagus*.'

Siti laughed. 'And one more word for you, Holly –

"*monyet*", which means monkey.'

I repeated that too, so that it would stick in my brain. That was three words already – only two to go.

Then I told her about Mr Pike's challenge, to try a durian – and this really got her laughing.

'What's so funny?' I said. 'Is it that horrible?'

'For Malaysians, it is a very famous fruit. Delicious.'

'Phew. So . . .'

'We say, "It smell like the toilet, it taste like heaven."'

I frowned, though at least the second bit sounded okay.

We eventually reached the cluster of trees. It was probably much too small to be called a jungle, but 'jungle' sounds very cool, so . . . we stepped into the jungle. There were forty or fifty tall trees, all with plenty of branches and leaves – but no monkeys. At least, I couldn't see any, though I did spot some monkey droppings. I was thinking about pointing them out to Siti, but she probably thought I was a bit weird anyway, without finding out that I was also an expert in animal poo.

Then she pointed up into a tree and whispered, '*Monyet!*'

At first I couldn't see anything.
Then a movement of black in the
high branches of a tree, a blur
of arms and legs . . . an actual
monkey! And then another one
nearby, swinging lazily from one
tree to another.

I didn't move at all – I didn't
want to disturb them, and Siti
was completely still too. Three
monkeys, then four. We watched
them in silence for ages. I could
tell from the look on Siti's face

how much she loved nature – she was completely at home here. I knew how she felt. She'd asked me only minutes ago if I liked monkeys, and I'd said 'not really'. But if she asked me again now, I would have told her that they were my all-time favourite animal. Because up close, in the wild, they were completely mesmerising.

We watched them until our necks ached.

The smallest monkey was swinging around and making an awful screechy noise, annoying the others – this monkey really reminded me of Emily Fellows.

Then an older one came along, glancing nervously about, stuffing its face with some kind of fruit, making a lot of noise and having a good old scratch. That one, of course, made me think of my dad.

*Dad!*

The hotel.

I pulled out my pocket watch.

12.30.

I gasped.

I'd been completely relaxed as I'd watched the monkeys – but that feeling vanished in a moment and now I felt sick – panicky, like Cinderella with the clock chiming midnight. But instead of a carriage turning into a pumpkin, it would be my dad, turning purple.

'I've got to get back,' I said breathlessly. '*Now*. Back at the hotel before one!'

But I'd said this too quickly. Siti hadn't understood. So I said it again – slower but just as panicky. Then she glanced at her watch and looked flustered too. 'I'm sorry,' she said. 'Let's go!'

We starting running back the way we came, snaking around trees and then back along the beach in the baking sun, already dripping with sweat. Running on sand is completely energy-sapping – I tried to keep up, but Siti was really fast. I stumbled and had to shout to her – she was metres ahead of me by now – that I needed a break. I was doubled over, panting, my heart thumping. She came back to me.

'You want to stop?'

I shook my head. I knew I had to keep going. I had no choice.

Siti led the way off the beach, back through the streets, past the banana man. Sweat was pouring off me by now – my T-shirt was soaked through. My feet

were pounding, my arms pumping, my mouth open –
I was trying to gulp as much air as possible (but no
insects).

By the time we reached her house, I was a wheezing,
hot, sweaty mess. Siti was out of breath too. She went
into the house and I stood outside, feeling abandoned,
not knowing whether to wait for her or try to find my
way back to the hotel alone.

I fumbled for my pocket watch. 12.49. My head hung.
It was hopeless.

It had taken us more than half an hour to walk back
to the hotel last night. There was no way I'd be able to
get back there in time, even if I wasn't so completely
exhausted. If by some miracle the trishaw man turned
up here right now, I'd still be late. My only hope was that
Dad would be late too.

But after a minute Siti came back outside, followed
by – I guessed – an older brother. He was tall, the same
height as Dad, and looked eighteen or nineteen. He was
carrying two motorbike helmets and gave one to me
and one to Siti. Then he hopped onto the motorbike –
without a helmet. Siti pointed to the seat behind him.

I got on without thinking and put my helmet on. It felt a bit loose. Siti got on after me. It was very squeezy.

Before I could say anything, her brother had started the engine, then revved the bike noisily and set off. I lurched backwards against Siti. She held on to me and I was clutching her brother's sides as if my life depended on it – because maybe it did. I'd never gripped anything so tightly – not even when I'd clung onto the tree on my tenth birthday at the start of the Dadventure. This was much more terrifying, like being on a rollercoaster – but one I wasn't at all sure I'd survive.

We wove through traffic, swerving and braking. Twice I thought we were going to crash. I clung on even tighter.

I'd never been as relieved as the moment when – over Siti's brother's left shoulder – I glimpsed the hotel. When we screeched to a halt in front of it, my body had stiffened so much that it took me a few seconds to move. Siti had got off but I just sat there trying to get my breathing back to normal. Then, after fumbling with the chinstrap, I took off my helmet and – finally – got off the bike. My thighs were aching from where they'd gripped the seat.

I squeaked my thanks to Siti's brother – in English, because the Malay way of saying it must have flown out of my brain on the motorbike ride – and handed the helmet to him. I nodded thanks to Siti but I didn't have time for a proper goodbye. I had to get to Adventure Club before Dad came back.

But when I looked towards the lobby of the hotel, my heart almost stopped.

Because there was Dad, staring at me, looking utterly shocked. And then completely furious.

# 9 Around the World in Eighty Plates

Dad was staring at me wide-eyed, but his mouth was all puckered up and his arms were tightly crossed in front of his chest. I walked over to him with a knot in my tummy.

Dad hardly ever lost his temper. He sometimes shouted at the referee when he was watching football on the telly, but he almost never got angry with non-referees, in real life. Still, I was fully expecting him to go completely nuts at me right now.

'Dad,' I mumbled, 'I'm really sorry . . .'

'Are you okay? Has anything bad happened to you?'

'No. I'm fine.'

He sighed with relief, then shook his head and said, 'Where . . . ?' But he couldn't finish the question, so he started another one instead. 'What . . . ?' Then he couldn't finish that one either. 'Why . . . ?'

I hung my head and bit my lip so that I wouldn't cry.

'Come on,' said Dad, and he turned and walked back into the hotel. I followed him through the lobby, into the lift and into our room. He didn't say one word the whole way. A few times he looked like he was about to speak, but then he shook his head, as if shaking the thought away, and sighed instead.

In the room, he pointed to my bed for me to sit down, and he sat at the end of his, but we weren't looking at each other – we were both facing the huge telly, which was turned off.

When Dad finally spoke, he actually sounded quite calm, but then I glanced at his face and it told a different story. His eyes were still angry, his nostrils flared, his lips really thin. 'So – where did you go?'

I told him everything. The words spilled out, but I was staring at my knees as I spoke: I couldn't look at him – couldn't bear the disappointment on his face. I tried to make my adventure seem as safe and natural as possible, like it hadn't been a crazy thing to do at all. I explained about missing breakfast and just popping outside and happening to bump into the same trishaw driver. I told Dad about what Mum had said last night on the phone, about going out and finding adventures. But I knew as I said all this how pathetic it must have sounded – like when Harrison forgot his homework and claimed that it had been completely shredded by his gerbil, Keith.

'What on earth were you thinking, Holly?' said Dad, and before I could answer he added, 'I was literally one minute away from calling the police. One minute! I'd been to Adventure Club, the room, the swimming pool, the beach. You're ten years old, for heaven's sake, in a new country, and you went off by yourself – without telling anybody – to an out-of-the-way place, to meet a girl you'd only met the night before – and you weren't even sure she would be there! Anything could've happened to you, Holly! Anything! And then – worst of all – you came back on a *motorbike*! Three people on one bike, ridden by some teenager that you'd never met. Do you know how incredibly dangerous that is?'

I just sat on my bed, looking at my knees, feeling completely terrible.

The atmosphere in our hotel room that afternoon was really tense. Dad was sighing and shaking his head a lot. I went for a shower, but even that didn't cheer me up. I hadn't put suncream on in the morning, so I'd got sunburnt, and the shower felt like thousands of tiny pins pricking my skin.

When I dried off and got dressed, Dad had changed into a new shirt and announced that we were going out for a walk on the beach.

Dad has a pretty terrible taste in clothes, but this shirt was something else. It was hard to look at it without squinting. Ms Devenport had once said that you should never look directly at the sun, because you might go blind – and this was also very good advice for Dad's shirt. It was silky, long-sleeved and very brightly coloured: blue, yellow, green, orange and red. There was a picture of a sun, a palm tree and a parrot, and it was easily the most embarrassing thing he'd ever worn – and this was a man who'd once gone to a fancy dress party wearing a rabbit onesie, waving around a massive inflatable carrot.

Normally I'd shake my head and ask him to please get changed – explaining that I just couldn't be seen in public next to him wearing such a horrible thing. But today I didn't feel like I could say anything. Maybe he secretly knew this. Maybe the shirt was Dad's secret weapon – his unusual way of punishing me.

We walked along the beach in silence, except for bird calls and the sound of waves lapping the shore. The sun was setting – the real sun, and unfortunately not the sun on Dad's shirt, which was still blazing. Then he squinted out to sea and pointed at Monkey Island in the distance.

'That's where I went this morning,' he said. 'On a speedboat, with six other travel writers. We landed on the beach – it was stunning. The company that owns our hotel is going to build a super-luxury hotel there.'

'Even more luxury than our one?' I asked, because I found that very hard to believe.

'Apparently so,' Dad said.

I shook my head in wonder. Maybe there would be *ten* different juices to choose from at breakfast, and the Egg Man would be *juggling* eggs and not just cooking them.

Maybe the lift would be supersonic and the showers would be like mini-waterfalls. Maybe there would be *boxes* of chocolates on each super-fluffy pillow.

'Siti told me that the locals call it Monkey Island, because there's loads of monkeys living there, and they'll have nowhere to go when they build the hotel – except to zoos.'

Dad frowned. 'Really?'

'That's what she said.'

'Because Jennifer – the hotel VP who went with us this morning – she didn't mention monkeys at all.'

'Siti also said that they have animals called "mouse deer" there.'

Dad shook his head. 'I don't think so. I read about them in the in-flight magazine – they're an endangered species.'

I looked at Dad and shrugged. 'You could always investigate. You *are* a journalist.'

He smiled like I was making a joke, but I really wasn't.

'There are lots of different types of journalist, Holly. There's the regular kind, who report the news – some of what they write is actually true, some of it's kind-of-true, and some of it –' he whispered the next bit – 'they completely make up.'

'Really?'

He nodded.

'Then there are investigative journalists – people who really try to get to the bottom of things. They often go undercover and put themselves in great danger to get a story.'

'That's exactly what I . . .'

'And finally,' he said, 'there is one more type of journalist – the kind that writes about daft things, like the time they got lost in a Brazilian rainforest, or the time they forgot about the cheese on toast that they'd left on the grill and almost burnt the house down.' (Dad had actually done both of those things.) 'Guess which kind I am, Holly.'

I sighed.

For years and years, I'd told pretty much everyone I know – and lots of people that I didn't know – that my dad was this great explorer. I'd been super-proud. And he'd definitely had exciting journeys over the years – to places that even *I* had never heard of, all over the world.

But these days he just didn't seem to be adventurous any more.

As we walked back along the beach, Dad produced a tennis ball from his pocket. He never went to the beach without one. 'When you have a tennis ball,' he always said, 'you can never be bored.' He threw it to me now, and we played 'classic catches' for a while. I think that this was his way of saying that I was forgiven – at least a bit.

After the beach, we went straight to the hotel restaurant for dinner. It was another buffet. This one was called 'Around the World in Eighty Plates'. There was pasta, paella and periperi chicken, and that was just the 'P's. There was sushi, curry, mini-hamburgers-in-buns and loads more.

Dad was never happier than when he was at a buffet. He took 'All You Can Eat' as a personal challenge. He even used tactics – no salad and no bread. And, without Mum here to make sure he wasn't going to eat his own bodyweight, he really got stuck in. When he eventually came back to our table, his plate was piled super-high – it was less like a meal and more like a food-based game of Jenga.

Dad was normally quite a messy eater – Mum was forever pointing out bits of rice or cheese that had got stuck in his beard, or spots of sauce or gravy that had splashed onto his clothes. The only good thing about his terrible new shirt was that it was excellent camouflage for spillages.

Watching Dad eat reminded me of the monkey from earlier, and that got me thinking about what Siti had said: about what would happen to all the monkeys on that island. It seemed so unfair. They'd been living there for years and years – centuries probably – just minding their own business. And now the trees where they lived would be chopped down and the monkeys themselves would be captured and locked up in zoos, all so that super-rich people could have an even more beautiful place where they could stuff their faces at All You Can Eat buffets.

Dad had a sweet-and-sour prawn on the end of his fork, but he must have seen me looking sad because he paused it in mid-air. 'What's up, Holly?'

'I was just thinking about the poor monkeys,' I said.

He popped the prawn into his mouth and chewed on

it, deep in thought. Then he swallowed, put down his fork and wiped his mouth, before pushing back his chair, standing up from the table, smiling and saying, 'Come with me.'

I did. I guessed that he was going to take me to the buffet to introduce me to a new kind of food from yet another country – there was probably something from Poland or Burkina Faso that he hadn't managed to squeeze onto his first plate. But no. To my horror, he walked over to the table where Patrick and his mum were having dinner.

Patrick already thought that I was an idiot. Seeing me now – with a sunburnt face, next to Dad in *that* shirt – would completely confirm it. Not that I particularly cared what he thought, but no one likes being laughed at, do they? Especially not by someone like Patrick.

His mum smiled at us as we approached her table, but he didn't even look up. He was wearing a baseball cap and had a plateful of mini-burgers. He shoved one into his mouth, but he was playing on his iPad at the same time. In the same way, his mum was tapping away on a laptop while nibbling at a salad. She was wearing a

red dress with matching lipstick and had perfect big hair like someone in a shampoo advert.

'Hi, Jennifer,' Dad said. She smiled, put down her cutlery, dabbed her lips with a napkin and squinted at Dad – possibly because she was dazzled by the shirt, or possibly because she was trying to remember his name.

'Jim,' he said.

'Of course. The one with the funny blog.'

'And this is my daughter, Holly.'

'Hello, Holly. This is Patrick. Say hello, Patrick.' He looked up from his screen for a millisecond and, when he saw it was me, scowled and grunted something that might have been 'hello'.

'Are you having a fun holiday, Holly?' she asked. 'Are you enjoying our hotel?'

'Yes, thank you.'

'Sorry to interrupt your meal,' said Dad. 'but I was just talking with Holly here, and I have a very quick question about the new hotel.'

'Fire away.'

'Holly was wondering what will happen to all the monkeys that live over there.'

Jennifer smiled, a really big one, and looked right into my eyes as she answered. 'That's a great question, young lady.' Her smile was so nice that I almost forgave the 'young lady' bit. 'I know that it's known locally as "Monkey Island",' she said, 'but there aren't actually that many monkeys there these days, I'm afraid – only a handful – and they'll all be moved to a safe place, where they'll be looked after, and fed, and happy.'

'Like a zoo?' I asked.

'Oh no,' she said, smiling again. 'More like a monkey sanctuary. Like a huge play area where they can hang out – literally, I suppose!'

She laughed at her own joke. Dad laughed too.

'I also heard that there are mouse deer on the island,' I said.

She grinned and looked at Dad.

'It seems like you've got a junior reporter in the family,' she said. Then she looked back at me. 'I heard that rumour too, Holly, about the mouse deer. So we did something called an "environmental impact survey" –' she made the quotation marks with her fingers in the air – 'and I'm happy to report there are no endangered animals of any kind there.'

'But—' I was about to tell her what Siti had said when Dad butted in.

'Ah, that's really good news,' he said. 'Thanks for putting her mind at rest. And apologies again for interrupting your meal.'

'Not at all,' said Jennifer.

We went back to our table and sat down.

'Young Patrick is quite the chatty one,' Dad said, smiling. 'That wouldn't be the same rude kid you were talking about earlier, would it?'

I nodded, but then I frowned, because I was really annoyed with Dad.

'I was about to tell her that there isn't just a handful of monkeys on the island. Siti said there are loads of them. And then I was going to ask her the name of the so-called "Monkey Sanctuary".'

'I guessed that you were going to do something like that,' he said quietly. 'That's why I stopped you.'

'So – do you believe that lady, and not Siti? Or is it that you don't want to cause any problems because we're not paying for this hotel?'

I couldn't hide my disappointment, but Dad shook his head and lowered his voice. 'Actually, it's neither of those things. Your friend Siti has no reason at all to tell fibs. But the company that owns this hotel has millions of reasons – think of all the money they'll make from the new place. But if people around the world knew about those monkeys and what will happen to them – or if there *are* endangered species over there – it might even stop the hotel from being built.'

Then Dad raised his eyebrows and leaned forward.

'Do you feel like a bit of investigating tomorrow?' he whispered.

# 10  The Plan

There were no sleep-ins the next day. When Dad pulled back the curtains, the sun was just coming up, and everything had an orangey-red glow. I looked out to sea, across to Monkey Island. Our plan was to go there, but we'd need help – and would need to be careful.

The call to prayer was coming from a mosque, and I got dressed, still half asleep. Dad was wearing the same shirt as last night, and I had to put on my brightest shirt too, an orange one, because it was my only long-sleeved top – to cover my sunburnt arms. Dad stuffed a pen and his reporter's notepad into his pocket and passed his phone to me.

'I need a snapper,' he said.

'Isn't that a fish?'

'Yes, it is – but it's also slang for a photographer,' he explained. 'Can you take the photos today?'

'Sure,' I said, glowing – it felt like we were a real team.

We took the lift down to the restaurant. I was too nervous to be super-hungry – I just had an omelette from Egg Man. But Dad was getting stuck into a big breakfast – basically a big plateful of fried food, and a small plate containing one Danish pastry which had a bit of apricot on top. Dad pointed to it proudly and said, 'Fruit,' as if it somehow made his breakfast healthy.

I was feeling a bit guilty about eating the hotel's food when we were going on a spying mission against them, and I mentioned this to Dad. He just shrugged and said, 'A free breakfast is a free breakfast, Lolly,' before shovelling more food into his mouth. I rolled my eyes, so he added, 'Plus, if the hotel's got nothing to hide – if Jennifer was telling the truth last night – then they've got nothing to worry about, have they?'

It was then that I spotted Patrick at the next table. I was surprised to see him, because he didn't seem like an early riser, and I hadn't noticed him when we'd walked

in. He was by himself with a large bowl of Coco Pops and he was on his iPad again. He glanced at me, scowled and went straight back to whatever he was doing on the screen.

If there was a competition for my least favourite kid in the world, the winner would still probably be Emily Fellows, but Patrick would definitely make the final.

After breakfast, Dad bought a big bottle of cold water from the hotel shop for our mission, and then we walked through the lobby. He told me to relax and pretend that we were just going out for an early morning stroll, and not to draw attention to ourselves. But our clothes made it pretty impossible for us to blend in.

It was really hot outside, even this early. Not many people were around but – incredibly – our trishaw driver was waiting in his usual spot in front of the hotel. Did he ever take a break? Did he actually *live* in his trishaw? I really hoped not.

'Hello, my friends,' he said. 'Same place?'

Dad nodded, and the driver gave us a really puzzled look, as if to say, *What is it about that street that you love so much?* followed by a big, toothless smile. 'Okay,' he said.

As he pedalled us along the usual route, I thought back to my previous trip and how wobbly I'd been feeling then – it was much nicer to have Dad next to me. He seemed to have forgiven me for yesterday and had this twinkle in his eyes which told me that he was still a great explorer at heart, after all.

After the trishaw man had dropped us off and Dad paid him, we walked to Siti's street. Everything here was pretty quiet, except for one very noisy cockerel. I led the way, because I knew my way around the area by now, though I still wasn't sure that I'd be able to recognise Siti's house. But when we got there it was unmistakable – her brother's motorbike was outside. Dad looked at it and shook his head. 'I can't believe you went on that death trap,' he muttered. 'And three of you too.'

So he hadn't completely forgiven me – not yet.

We stood side by side on their front step and he knocked on the door.

Siti's dad answered it, wearing a sarong and no top, and when he saw us he was really surprised. I could completely understand why – the last time he'd seen us was when he'd cooked that delicious fried rice for us two nights ago. And yet here we were at his front door unannounced, first thing in the morning. It was a wonder he didn't call the police.

'*Selamat pagi*,' said Dad, which I later found out was 'good morning'.

'*Selamat pagi*,' replied Siti's dad – frowning – and then he turned and shouted for Siti. She rushed over in her school uniform – a white and dark-blue dress – and when *she* looked really shocked to see us too, I was completely regretting coming.

She looked at my dad, bowed her head and said, 'I am very sorry, sir.'

'Sorry for what?' asked Dad.

'For being late with Holly yesterday. You are very angry?'

'No,' said Dad. 'No, no, no. No, no, no, no, no.' Which was a lot of 'no's. Of course, it wasn't Siti he'd been angry with.

'We're here about Monkey Island,' I explained.

'Monkey Island?'

'I told Dad about it last night. About the monkeys and what's going to happen to them. He's a journalist,' I added proudly, though I'm sure I'd told her this a few times already. 'He spoke to a manager at the hotel last night, but she told him that there were only a *few* monkeys there. So we want to investigate. To find out the truth. To visit the island and look for ourselves, so Dad can write about it. He thinks that if there is a lot of wildlife there, and if lots of people know about this, it might save the island from the hotel.'

Siti gave me a puzzled look. 'Can you say that again, but slower?'

I winced. Nodded. Then I tried again less excitably, and this time she understood, and translated it for her dad.

Meanwhile, the hallway had got really crowded. Some of Siti's brothers and sisters were there, as well as a grandfather and Siti's mum (wearing a headscarf). They'd all come to see what was happening. Everyone listened to Siti, but as soon as she finished they all started talking – at the same time, pretty much. It looked like what my dad calls 'an animated discussion', and what my mum calls 'an argument'. But they eventually seemed to agree on something and Siti turned to us.

'My family say please come in.'

In the front room of their house there was a TV, a sofa, two armchairs, a low table with a pedestal fan, and a huge rug on the concrete floor. The rug was really colourful – like Dad's shirt, except a lot more tasteful.

I sat next to Dad on the sofa. Siti's dad and granddad sat in the armchairs, her mum went to make the drinks, and everyone else just stood around. The motorbike brother from yesterday was there – his name was Ahmed. Siti sat down next to me on the sofa, looking a lot more relaxed now she knew she wasn't in trouble.

Dad had an iced coffee (and whispered to me that it was so strong he'd probably be awake until Christmas). I had another chocolate milk, which was just as good as the one I'd had the other night. And, with loads of the family talking, and Siti mostly translating (though her brothers and sisters knew some English too), they explained what was happening at Monkey Island. Dad took out his notepad and pen and started taking notes like a real journalist.

'The company say that local people want this new hotel because it makes more jobs,' Siti explained. 'But we *don't* want it. Nobody does. We have many hotels here already, but we have not so many beautiful islands. And there are not "a few" monkeys there. There are hundreds. We have seen them. Other animals too. We visit the island in a boat ourselves – many times. But the hotel will *chop* the trees and take the monkeys and other animals. My sister – who works at the hotel as a cleaner – she says that everyone knows the monkeys will be sold to zoos or even pet shops.'

Then there was silence. Everyone was looking at my dad.

'Is there a way of getting there without being noticed?' he asked.

Siti translated his question, which started another noisy discussion.

'They are saying that my uncle has a boat,' said Siti eventually. 'We can call him and ask him to take you to the island. But – not to the main beach, because the hotel people will see you and stop you. He will take you to a place where people usually don't go.'

'Like a back entrance?' said Dad.

She nodded. 'But it might be difficult to reach the monkeys from there. They live mostly in the middle of the island, away from the sea. My brother Ahmed can join you but not today – he has to work. My father too.'

Dad shook his head. 'No – I don't want to get any of you into trouble.' He looked at me. 'And it sounds like it might be too dangerous for you, Holly.'

I stared at him as if he'd completely lost his mind. This was the adventure I'd been waiting my whole entire life for!

Dad hesitated and there was an awful moment when I thought he was about to call the whole thing off. Or put me into Adventure Club while he investigated alone.

But he didn't.

Siti's dad called the uncle, and it was all arranged; we could go straight away. The uncle would take us to the island and then come back to pick us up in the early afternoon. I put Siti's dad's mobile number into our phone, in case of emergency.

We were about to get up to leave when there was a knock at the door. Everyone stopped, and in stepped one of the little boys from yesterday – the 'one-two-three-four-five' kid. We were all staring at him as he said something excitedly in Malay – something that got a nervous reaction and started another big family discussion. Siti translated for us.

'He says that two men wearing hotel uniforms are at the end of this street, on a motorbike, watching our house. My father thinks they must be here to stop you getting to the island.' She shook her head sadly. 'They followed you here.'

The family was still
discussing this new
information and there
was a lot of head-shaking.

Dad sighed and looked
at me. 'If the hotel has
sent people to follow
us,' he said, 'it's actually
a really good sign, in a way –
it means that we must be on
to something. Jennifer must have got suspicious after
our questions last night and asked security at the hotel
to keep an eye on us.'

I shook my head.

'Patrick,' I said. I should have known that he was up
to something this morning. 'That's what he was doing at
breakfast – spying on us! Maybe he even overheard our
plans. He probably used his iPad to let his mum know
where we were.'

Dad groaned. 'And, with hindsight, it probably didn't
help that we're wearing these shirts, or that we came
here by the slowest possible form of transport, other

than a donkey. A blind man could probably have tailed us.'

But I had an idea. I remembered what Mr Pike had taught me in our last session – about misdirection. Breathlessly, I explained my plan to Dad and Siti, and she translated it for her family.

Dad was waggling his head, as if weighing it all up. He seemed impressed though. 'It *could* work,' he said.

Then Siti's dad looked at me, rubbed his chin and said, '*Bagus*.'

# 11  Journey to Monkey Island

I got changed in Siti's bedroom. It was really small – two single beds, a desk and a wardrobe were crammed in there. The wall next to Siti's bed had three posters – a rock band I'd never heard of, an old Spider-Man movie, and one of a cute fluffy kitten poking out of a boot. I took off my orange top and put on a baggy pale green shirt that Siti lent me. Then Dad got changed in the bathroom, swapping his terrible shirt for a plain blue T-shirt belonging to Ahmed. It was a pretty tight fit, but Dad didn't seem to mind. 'As long as I don't breathe,' he said, 'it'll be fine.'

Siti put my orange top over her uniform and Ahmed put on Dad's shirt. Poor Ahmed. He'd swapped a perfectly decent T-shirt for Dad's crime-against-fashion. At least it was only for one day.

The rest of the family looked at us all and seemed to find the whole thing hilarious. The granddad in particular was rocking with laughter and slapping his thigh.

Siti wished me luck and smiled – she seemed happy to be having an adventure too. Then she and Ahmed put on motorbike helmets and left the house. The rest of us sat in silence, waiting.

The plan – my plan – was to fool the hotel security guards into thinking that the people on the motorbike were us, and so they'd follow Ahmed and Siti on a wild goose chase. Eventually, Ahmed would drop Siti off at her school and the guards would realise that they'd been tricked – but by then Dad and I would already be on the island.

We listened to the motorbike as Ahmed revved it up and rode away, and then we waited some more. The boy came back, whooping with delight – the hotel men had taken the bait. There was clapping and cheering from the family. I was beaming. The plan had worked! Or the first bit had, at least.

Siti's dad stood up, gestured for Dad and me to follow him, and then the three of us left the house in a hurry. We didn't know how long it would be before the men realised that they were following the right shirts but the wrong people. Maybe only a minute or two. So we had no time to waste.

Siti's dad had this shuffling run which didn't look quick, but it was surprisingly hard to keep up with him. I was panting, Dad was wheezing and we were both dripping with sweat by the time we reached the small beach. A man was waiting in a small wooden boat which was bobbing gently in shallow water. It had a motor on the back.

I knew it was Siti's uncle straight away. He looked almost exactly like her dad, except that his facial hair was even more impressive – the kind of moustache you'd expect a circus strongman to have.

When we reached the shore, the brothers said a few urgent words to each other – there was a lot of nodding and head-waggling and pointing – and then Siti's dad held the boat steady so Dad and I could clamber in.

The uncle started the motor, and we were off, leaving Siti's dad behind us on the shore.

Everything had been quiet and still on the beach but the motor was noisy and raspy, and we went surprisingly fast. The cool breeze swept my hair back and dried the sweat on my face. I gripped my seat. Every time the front end of the boat lifted into the air and slapped back down against the water, I felt my bones rattling and concentrated on not being sick. But Dad looked like he was having the best time ever. He was holding on tightly too, but grinning. He'd definitely got his sense of adventure back.

It only took us a few minutes to get there, though it felt like much longer. Siti's uncle really slowed down as we got close, because there were sharp rocks and tree stumps jutting out of the water near the shore. He was muttering under his breath and it was probably a good thing that we didn't speak Malay.

He nudged the boat between two rocks and edged close enough to the shore for Dad to grab a branch that was overhanging the water.

This place didn't look at all inviting – dark, with craggy rocks, trees at strange angles and no path. Scary, yes – but definitely a place for an adventure.

I stood up in the boat very carefully – Dad steadied me – then I grabbed the branch, wobbled and took a breath, before swinging and planting my feet on the island. I teetered backwards and let out a little squeak, but managed to stay on my feet – just. Phew. Then Dad tried the same thing, except that the branch bent lower under his weight – he almost lost his balance, yelped and

was really close to having an unexpected swim – but he clung on desperately, stretched a leg out and scrambled onto the island next to me. For a pair of explorers, we were both really clumsy.

Siti's uncle fished our big bottle of water from under his seat and tossed it to Dad.

Then he held up one finger, before pointing at his wrist. It was like a game of charades, and I completely love charades. But I don't think he was miming a TV show or a movie or a book, unless it was one word and called something like 'Wrist'.

Dad guessed the answer, which was, 'Meet back here at one.'

Siti's uncle pointed again – towards the centre of the island – and said, '*Monyet.*'

'Monkeys,' I explained to Dad, really proud that another of my four Malay words had come in handy. 'He's telling us where the monkeys are.'

Then, without another word, Siti's uncle carefully turned the boat around and headed off – we shouted to thank him, but it was drowned out by the sound of the motor. We watched the boat get smaller and smaller. I looked at Dad. He'd been super-confident all morning, but now he was frowning and shaking his head.

'What's up?' I asked.

'This – coming here – was maybe the worst idea I've ever had. And I've had some really terrible ideas.' This was true: only last week, for example, he'd come up with something called 'Kanga-shoes' – trainers with springs in the heels that let you bounce everywhere.

'But coming here was a great idea, Dad,' I said. 'One of your absolute best.'

He shook his head again. 'We're in a foreign country, Holly, on private property. It looks like difficult terrain, and it seems that powerful people want to stop us from investigating. I'm getting too old for all this stuff, and you're still too young.'

'I'm not a little kid any more, Dad – you said that yourself. And I wanted to come here – you didn't make me. We're having an actual adventure! A real one. Doing something important!'

Dad took a deep breath. 'If I don't tell Mum about the motorbike, you don't tell her about this. Deal?'

'Deal,' I said, but we both knew that Mum would find out soon enough – she was impossible to keep secrets from. One look from her, and we'd both be confessing everything.

'Come on then,' Dad said. 'Stay close.'

# 12  Monkey Business

Siti hadn't been kidding. It wouldn't be easy to get to the middle of the island from here. In fact, it might even be impossible. We'd been going for ten long minutes and hadn't got far at all, scrambling over rocks and scraping past trees and bushes. We'd only travelled fifty metres and we'd already seen a green snake as long as my arm and some kind of lizard that was even bigger than that. Both of these things made me yelp.

It was still hot and sticky, but at least the trees were shading us from the fierce sun. Dad passed the water bottle to me, and I took a long swig.

Dad's shirt (which was actually Ahmed's shirt, but you know what I mean) was completely soaked with sweat and had turned from light blue to dark blue.

'The more I think about it,' he said, wiping sweat from his forehead, 'the more I miss the air-con in our hotel room.'

I knew how he felt. I missed that too, and the shower and the pillows – everything. Monkey Island was spectacular, and real, but it was also incredibly uncomfortable.

'I'm starting to think that Jennifer was right after all,' he said. 'Maybe there are only one or two monkeys here. Or they're all incredibly good at hiding.'

Dad was looking up into the branches for any sign of movement, but I was concentrating on the ground. That's how I noticed the monkey poo. I pointed it out excitedly to Dad, who nodded and said, 'Monkey business. Get it?'

There really was no situation where Dad wouldn't try to make a terrible joke.

I soon found another monkey dropping, and another and another. It was everywhere. I followed the trail of monkey poo, which was a bit like following a trail of breadcrumbs, except much stinkier.

After a few minutes, Dad said, 'Either there *are* a lot of monkeys here, or it's one monkey with some very serious tummy problems.'

Very soon we had the answer.

We scrambled down a bank and then over a small mound and –

I gasped.

Dad said, 'Wow.'

There were monkeys everywhere – dozens of them: some were sitting in trees, others swinging from branches or climbing or chasing each other. The whole place was writhing with monkey activity.

'How many do you think there are?' whispered Dad.

I tried to count them, but it was much harder to count monkeys than coins or apples or shells because those other things don't keep leaping on top of each other.

'Thirty-four,' I said eventually. 'Though I might have counted some of them twice. Or missed some.'

'And that's only the ones in this small clearing,' said Dad, wide-eyed. 'There must be loads more. Hundreds, probably.'

I got the phone out and took some photos, trying to stay quiet and still so that I didn't disturb them. Then Dad whispered for me to make a short video to put on his blog – which was fine, except he started directing me like he was Steven Spielberg.

'First, a wide shot, a few seconds of the monkeys doing monkey-ish things. Then pan to me – I'll say a few words. Then swing back for a bit more monkey action. Then . . . cut.'

I started recording. When I turned to film Dad, he put on this different voice – serious and whispery like he was a wildlife presenter on the telly.

'Here we are on Monkey Island. It's the site of a new super-luxury hotel to be built by the Can-Asian Hotels Group. But, to build it, many of these trees – and all of their monkey inhabitants – will have to be removed. The hotel claims that, despite the name, only a few monkeys call this island home. In just this one small area, however, we've already counted thirty-four. Locals say there are hundreds.'

He nodded, which was my signal to turn and film the monkeys for a few more seconds. Then I stopped recording. We both watched the video I'd made.

'Nice camerawork,' said Dad. 'Very steady. You're a natural.'

Then we both stood and watched the monkeys some more. They were definitely my new favourite animal.

When I got back home, I'd let my grandparents know this, because once, when I was little, they'd all taken me to the zoo and I'd gone nuts for the penguins. So, pretty much every birthday or Christmas since then, they'd got me something penguin-y. It would make a nice change to get monkey-related presents for a while.

As we watched the monkeys though, one of them shrieked, then some others, and there was a sudden flurry of movement in the trees. I looked at Dad, eyebrows up.

'Maybe they've noticed us,' I whispered.

But it wasn't us that had startled them – we heard voices! Loud ones. There were people, not far away. Two men, it sounded like. We both frantically looked around, though we couldn't see anyone yet. But their voices were getting louder. And they were coming this way.

'We need to hide,' whispered Dad. *Fast.*

Up to now I'd actually felt safe, despite everything, because Dad was here. But the panicky look on his face now really worried me, and so did the way he nearly pulled my arm out of its socket as he steered me over to a thick bush.

'Ow!' I whispered.

'Sorry,' he whispered back.

We wriggled inside the bush, scraping ourselves on its sharp branches.

'Ow!' I whispered again.

'Sorry.'

Then we sat side by side trying not to make a sound, knees under our chins, feet tucked tightly in.

We could see out of the bush – just – which meant that someone would be able to spot us if they looked closely enough. At least we weren't wearing our own shirts. That was one good thing.

Dad sighed, and whispered, 'This is definitely the worst thing I've ever done as a parent. I can't believe I'm putting you in danger like this.' He shook his head. 'This is even worse than the time that I dropped you.'

'You dropped me?' I whispered back.

'Well,' he explained, 'it was more of a fumble.'

'You make me sound like a football.'

'You weren't much bigger than one actually. You were just a baby.'

'You dropped a baby?'

'I'd picked you up out of the bath. You were surprisingly slippy.'

'It's surprising to you? That soap and water make things slippy?'

'But it was fine – you landed in the tub, in the water, on your bottom. Which was really well padded, at the time. You were a really chubby baby, Holly. You had chubby cheeks – both upper and lower.'

I couldn't believe that, at a moment like this – as we were hiding in a bush, completely terrified – Dad was making a joke about my bottom.

'Did I cry?'

'You actually laughed, like it was some kind of game. That's when I knew I had a little adventurer in the family.'

'I can't believe you actually dropped me.'

'It was a long time ago, Holly,' he whispered. 'And this is much, much worse.'

Then neither of us spoke, because the voices got nearer, and the two men walked towards us: a stocky one and a tall skinny one. Both were wearing khaki shirts, shorts and walking boots, and the short man had a walkie-talkie. It looked like they were coming straight for us – I couldn't breathe – but then it seemed that they were going to walk on by. As they were only two steps past our bush though, the walkie-talkie crackled. They stopped, and my heart almost stopped too. A loud voice came through the walkie-talkie. It was unmistakable: Patrick's mum. Jennifer.

'They're not at the hotel – haven't been back to their room. Our best guess is that they're currently on the island. Over.'

The short man held the walkie-talkie in front of his mouth and said in an American accent, 'Can you repeat the description? Over.'

'He's a middle-aged man – tall, a bit flabby, glasses. A ridiculous goatee beard. The girl is about nine, short hair, tomboyish. Over.'

'If they're here,' said the man, 'we'll sniff them out. When we do, what action do you want us to take? Over.'

'They're trespassing on private property – so, detain them. Take their cameras or phones, if they have them, and delete all photos. If they have any evidence at all of the wildlife, that would not be good. Alert me immediately, and call the police if they don't cooperate. Over and out.'

I gasped – I just couldn't help it.

The two men looked at each other and had a muttered conversation. Then they turned this way. I was certain that they'd heard me gasp.

I scrunched my eyes shut and waited to be captured.

# 13  Tarzan

I was trying to breathe without making any kind of sound – which is really hard to do when you're completely terrified.

A monkey screeched. It sent shivers through me, but the men turned away from our bush to look for it. The monkey must have been doing something funny, because they both laughed, and then the tall one said something to the shorter one, and they both walked off – in the direction of our meeting point.

The men's footsteps got quieter and quieter and finally I felt safe enough to sigh and look at Dad, whose eyebrows were way up high – I didn't know eyebrows could go that far.

'That was close,' he whispered.

'Do you *think*?' I whispered back, proving that my sarcasm could operate even at highly stressful times.

Dad's sense of humour was obviously still working too. 'The good news,' he said, 'is they're looking for some other people. Middle-aged? Flabby? Could a flabby middle-aged person fit into this T-shirt? I wonder,' he said, looking down at his tummy.

I hadn't exactly been overjoyed to be called tomboyish either – or nine years old! – but we had much more important things to think about right now. Like getting off the island, and not being caught.

Neither of us dared to move out from the bush yet though. It felt oddly safe in here. Like we were invisible. We couldn't stay here forever but, as soon as we stepped out, we'd be in danger again.

Dad wriggled a bit, pulled the notepad and pen from his pocket and started scribbling something down. I shook my head. Incredible. I just couldn't believe that he was coming up with ideas here, right now. Even for Dad, this was a really inappropriate time.

'Can't it wait?' I snapped.

'I'm just taking down what Jennifer said,' Dad whispered, 'before I forget.' He obviously still hadn't got over her description. 'Flabby indeed! We'll show her what flabby men and their tomboyish nine year-old daughters can do.'

Just then there was movement – something on the ground just outside the bush. A small scratchy sound, but our ears were super-sensitive at that moment, and it made both of us jolt.

Not a person. An animal. And not a monkey. Something much smaller.

I looked at Dad, and his expression mirrored mine: complete bewilderment. Then I looked back at the animal. I was certain that this was what Siti had been talking about: it was just like a miniature deer!

Very slowly, very quietly, I pulled the phone from my pocket, turned on the camera and filmed the mouse deer as it sniffed the ground just outside our bush. It had tiny hooves, like a regular deer! It must have sensed us, because suddenly it skittered away – like a mouse!

'Wow,' said Dad. He asked me to pass him the phone, and watched my footage, grinning. 'That's the evidence we need. The monkeys were great, but the mouse deer is the icing on the cake!' Then he tapped the screen a few times and groaned.

'What?'

'There's no mobile coverage here. I need to send those photos and videos to my email so it won't matter if they delete them from the phone. But it's just not possible. And even worse, we can't call Siti's dad to change the meeting point.'

'Why do we need to do that?'

'Because we can't go back the way we came – that's the direction those two just went off in.' Dad hung his head. 'I'm sorry, Holly – for all *this*. The hiding-in-a-bush. The heat. The danger. The whole breaking-the-law thing. I wanted you to have exciting adventures – but PG-rated ones. This is too much. And we might even be stranded here.'

'Stranded?'

He nodded. 'If we miss the boat and can't contact anyone.'

I smiled. 'It'll be like *Nim's Island*,' I said enthusiastically. 'I'll be Nim and you can be the dad. Or like *The Jungle Book*. I'll be Mowgli. You can be Baloo. You've definitely got the tummy for it.'

'*Hey.*'

'Or we can make friends with the monkeys and swing from the trees. Like Tarzan.'

Dad tried to beat his chest with his fists, but his heart wasn't in it, so I said, 'That was rubbish, Dad. *I'll* be Tarzan. You can be Jane.'

Dad was usually the one who tried to find the positive in any situation. Not right now though. 'We've got half a bottle of warm water and no food, Holly. Being stuck here isn't going to be a game.'

*Stuck*. That word reminded me of something Ms Devenport had said. I'd been struggling with a question in maths one time, and told her that I was stuck. 'There's no such thing as "stuck",' she said, and showed me a different way of working the problem out. So, here in the bush, I took the notepad and pen from Dad, turned to an empty page and sketched a line drawing of the island, with two routes. The first route was the way that we'd come. The second way would hopefully still get us to the same meeting point, but avoiding the two men.

Dad nodded. 'There'll be more climbing that way though,' he said. 'And it's longer, so we might miss the boat.'

'We better get going then,' I said, and he must have seen the determined look on my face.

'You definitely take after your mum,' he said. 'You're a force of nature, Holly.' Then he smiled and we both wriggled out of the bush.

I scraped myself – again – and, not for the first time today, whispered, 'Ow.'

We tried not to make any noise, though we were both soon panting. We couldn't do anything about that: it was hot and we were exhausted. But we made quick progress for a while, until we were surrounded – not by men or monkeys but by crammed-together trees on both sides, and no way of getting through them. In front of us was a rock face that was ten times my height.

I looked at Dad. There were only two ways out – one was to retrace our steps, and we didn't have time for that.

The other option was to climb.

# 14  The Fear of Heights

One of the main reasons that my dad had planned the original Dadventure was to help me overcome my fear of heights. It was all because of the school trip to Mount Never-rest, the indoor climbing centre, where I'd panicked halfway up and needed to be talked down by the instructor.

Emily Fellows and her gang had found this completely hilarious, and school became unbearable for a while. Dad, rather than ignoring my humiliation like a normal parent might have done, or talking about it like Mum had done, had instead challenged me to climb Lofty – the name we'd given to the tallest tree in our garden. I know he was only trying to get me to face my fears and build up my confidence, but it was a bit like taking someone who was scared of snakes and throwing them into a snake pit. Wearing a mouse costume.

I'd eventually managed to climb to the top of Lofty, but I'd been wearing safety equipment and it had still been scary. Plus, it hadn't worked, not really, because I was still pretty scared of heights – just not absolutely terrified of them any more.

But this rock face would be tougher than Lofty *and* the wall at the rock-climbing centre combined. My palms were already slippy with sweat, my sunburn was throbbing and my whole body ached.

I looked at Dad and he must have known what I was thinking: he must have seen the panic in my eyes.

'We're going back,' he said. 'It's not worth the risk. If anything happened to you, Lolly . . .'

But he didn't get to finish, because I was already scrambling up the rock. The first bit was fairly easy – there were decent footholds and, even if I lost grip, it wasn't far to fall. But then about halfway up it got really tricky. My muscles tightened and my breathing got fast and shallow as I desperately looked for the next handhold.

'Come down if you're stuck,'
said Dad, but I shook my
head: *no such thing as 'stuck'.*
I moved my right hand up to
the next hold, gripped it with
my fingertips, moved my left
foot to another hole, and hung
on with my toes. Watching
those monkeys climb must
have helped me somehow. I
kept going, full of confidence
now, only two metres from the
top. I didn't dare look down,
but I said something just loud
enough for Dad to hear.

'Take a photo.'

'What?'

'Or – even better – a video.
Of me climbing. Please.'

I gave him a few seconds,
then said, 'Are you filming?'

'Yep.'

I wanted evidence – to show Emily Fellows and the others that I could do it. So I took a breath and kept on climbing, one careful movement at a time, and eventually I was close enough to scramble over the top.

I lay there for a few seconds, overcome with relief, and then I looked down at Dad. I was so glad I hadn't done that while I was still climbing. I felt dizzy. It was a long way down.

Dad threw the water bottle up to me and I grabbed it first time – a classic catch. And then he climbed up. He'd done a lot of climbing before and had long arms and legs, which really helped, but it still wasn't easy for him.

When he got to the top, he panted, 'Not bad for a flabby middle-aged guy.'

'With a ridiculous beard,' I added.

'Hey.'

We shared a smile.

'Great job, Holly. I'm completely proud of you.'

But we didn't have time for this. I checked my pocket watch – it was nearly one o'clock. We really had to hurry. Dad led the way. At one point he actually swung from a branch, like Tarzan (although the noise that came out of his mouth was less of a blood-curdling roar and more of a panicky squeal).

It wasn't long before we heard the sea lapping, so we knew that we must be close to the shore – but by this time we were already late. What if Siti's uncle had been and gone? What if those two men were waiting for us instead?

When we reached the shoreline, we both groaned: we were in the wrong place.

Through the trees and across the water, we could just make out the meeting place – but it was a hundred metres away and there was no easy way of getting there from here. Siti's uncle was sitting there in his boat. He was waiting, but for how much longer?

We waved to get his attention – flapping our hands wildly above our heads – but he wasn't looking this way and, even if he was, he might not have been able to spot us through the trees. So we did something incredibly risky.

'Hey!' Dad yelled, and I started shouting too. 'Over here!'

We kept on waving our arms and yelling. We knew

that it was possible – probable even – that the two men would hear us, but it was a risk we had to take.

It didn't work though. We just couldn't get Siti's uncle's attention.

Then I had an idea. On our last adventure, in the woods, Dad had taught me how to whistle super-loudly – with my fingers in the corners of my mouth – and that's what I did now. Dad did the same. Siti's uncle turned straight away and stared in our direction. Then he must have finally glimpsed us waving crazily, because he pushed the boat away from the shore, turned it around, got the motor going and headed towards us.

He was going as fast as he could, but the coastline was tricky to navigate and he seemed to be moving in slow motion. It was really frustrating. And scary, because the two men must have heard our whistles too, and we didn't know how close they were.

The next few minutes were the tensest moments of my entire life: I had to remember to breathe. I was watching Siti's uncle manoeuvring the boat, edging closer to us. Dad was staring inland, in case the men came, though I didn't know what we'd do if they got here first, because there was nowhere for us to go except into the water, and it was too deep for wading – plus we'd wreck my pocket watch and Dad's phone (and lose all the evidence – the photos and videos).

Then our boat was almost within touching distance, but it was really tricky for him to get in to shore – the waves were trying to push him off course, into a jagged rock. He was muttering and shaking his head, but eventually managed to reach us. The whole time, we were glancing over our shoulders to make sure the men weren't coming. Dad bundled me into the boat and Siti's uncle steadied me. Then Dad got in – very clumsily, of course, as you'd expect from a man who'd once dropped a baby – and we sat breathlessly, side by side.

Dad leaned out of the boat, helped push it out and we motored away. We looked back at Monkey Island, expecting to see the two men emerging and standing there, out of breath, shaking their fists at us like characters in a movie. But no one was there. Dad and I looked at each other, completely relieved, grinning. Then he hugged me – a real bone-cruncher. My heart was thumping in my chest. I could feel that Dad's was too.

# 15 Exclusive!

Before we got out of the boat, Dad shook Siti's uncle's hand, and we both said 'Terima kasih' to him – a lot. Then Dad and I clambered out onto the beach and pushed the boat back out to sea. Siti's uncle motored off. We were alone again.

Dad checked his phone and saw that we had reception now – so he uploaded our photos and videos to make sure that they were safe.

'Now what?' I asked.

'I'll email the newspaper to tell them the story. And then I'll write my blog, to get the information out into the world. But first, let's find something to drink. And a bite to eat. I'm starving.'

I shook my head in complete wonder. Only Dad could have an appetite straight after that bumpy boat ride, and so soon after all the tension of Monkey Island.

But by the time we found a food court – an open-air square with lots of tables in the middle, and ten different food stalls around the outside – I was hungry and thirsty too. We sat down and Dad ordered drinks. These didn't come in cups though, but two big green coconuts, which a man pulled out of a massive fridge. He hacked the tops off with the kind of knife you'd expect a pirate to own,

popped a straw in each coconut and presented them to us.

We slurped the cold coconut milk, and Dad emailed the newspaper: the subject was 'Exclusive!'

We ordered food and, while we waited, Dad went to his blog and was about to start tapping away when he seemed to change his mind. I frowned. Was he having second thoughts about writing the story? Was he chickening out at the last minute?

I needn't have worried.

'It's your challenge from Ms Devenport, isn't it?' he said. 'To write a blog?'

I nodded. I'd been planning to do it as soon as I got home. But now Dad passed me his phone.

'You write it, Holly. It's your story after all. You got the lead. You were the one who had the persistence, who found the monkeys, who avoided the hotel people, who took the pictures. So – you come up with the words, and I'll put the videos and photos in. And help you with editing and spelling, if you need it.'

And that's how I wrote my first ever blog:

# Holly's Holly-Day Diary
## The Monkey Island Investigation
*By Holly Chambers (age 10¾)*

Today my dad and I have been working as investigative journalists on Monkey Island. A super-posh hotel is going to be built there, and lots of trees will have to be chopped down. The company responsible – Can-Asian Hotels Group – says that there are no endangered species on the island, and only a few monkeys. But our investigation found something altogether different.

**This video** shows the truth about the monkeys on Monkey Island.

And **here** is an endangered species that we were lucky enough to see up close – it's called a mouse deer. It's actually a kind of deer, but it could fit

in a lunchbox!
**Warning:** *this clip contains literally the most adorable animal ever.*

Being an investigative journalist is hard work. **Here's a clip** of me climbing a steep rock face on the way back. (Mum: please don't watch this video!) (Emily Fellows: watch it and weep!)

So, as our investigation shows, there are lots of monkeys there – possibly hundreds – and at least one endangered species! There are already lots of great hotels around here. The question that the locals are asking is – why ruin a beautiful island, with all this incredible wildlife, for the sake of yet another hotel?

* * *

Dad checked it for mistakes, put in the videos and linked to it from his own blog. And then – perfect timing – our food arrived.

After we'd eaten – *wonton mee*, exotic food number three, a clear soup with noodles and these dumplings which were like little grenades of deliciousness – we walked back to our hotel in the hot sun, not sure of the welcome that we'd get when we stepped inside.

What happened was this: Patrick was waiting for us in the lobby, sitting in an armchair like he was a baddy in a James Bond movie and clutching his iPad (which I was starting to think he might actually be glued to). As soon as he saw us, he sprang up and dashed off – then came back seconds later with his mum and a really large security guy.

Dad patted my shoulder and whispered, 'It's fine, Holly. Leave it to me.'

Jennifer didn't give us a big smile this time. Instead, her lips were a thin line and her eyes were narrow.

'Where have you two been, I wonder?' she asked.

'Out and about,' Dad replied cheerfully. 'Exploring.'

'I gathered that,' she said. 'From your blog, which I've noticed has just been updated.'

Patrick held out the iPad, looking smug. My blog post was on the screen. I think I was meant to feel caught out, but I just felt super-proud. Those were my words out there in the world, from our investigation!

Dad looked slightly sheepish. 'Well, I had such a nice time at Monkey Island yesterday,' he said, 'that I wanted to take Holly there.'

'And we saw some things that you didn't show Dad yesterday,' I added. 'Like all the monkeys and some other animals too. Endangered ones.'

She glared at us.

'And for your information,' Dad said, rubbing his chin, 'there are plenty of beards that are more ridiculous than this one.'

'Plus I'm nearly eleven, thank you very much. Also, just because I don't wear dresses, it doesn't make me a tomboy.'

Jennifer looked awkward for a moment, realising what must have happened, but then she recovered.

'You've got ten minutes to pack your bags,' she said icily. Patrick tapped and swiped the screen of his iPad and showed it to us – he'd already started the countdown clock and was smirking.

Dad stayed calm and pleasant. 'But you can't make us leave, can you?' he said. 'We haven't actually broken any hotel rules.'

'You're absolutely right,' she said. 'We can't make you go. But from now on, if you do wish to stay, you'll be staying as paying guests – our rate is $800 a night. You can settle up at reception.'

Dad winced and looked at me.

'I think we'll pack our bags,' he said.

'Good idea,' she said. 'And don't go thinking that you've changed the world. Luckily hardly anyone bothers to read that blog of yours.'

The security man joined Dad and me in the lift. He looked incredibly strong. Even his fingers looked muscly, and his neck was so wide that it was hard to tell where the neck finished and the head started. He waited outside our room, arms crossed, while we packed. I really wanted a shower – I was dirty, a bit smelly and sticky with dried sweat. It was really frustrating, knowing that such an incredible shower was only steps away but that there was no time to use it.

Dad swiped the complimentary toothbrushes and little bottles of shampoo as a small act of revenge, stuffing them into his rucksack, and then we left. The security guy joined us in the lift again – he wasn't much of a talker – and escorted us through the lobby, where Jennifer was glaring and Patrick was gloating and waving us goodbye.

We stepped outside into the heat, dragging our heavy bags. I'd been feeling incredibly happy since we'd come back from the island: we'd had a brilliant – if terrifying – adventure, and our mission had been accomplished. But seeing the look on Patrick's face, I thought maybe *they'd* won after all. Maybe nobody *was* going to read our blog, and nothing would change for the animals: they'd still lose their habitat. And we'd just lost ours – kicked out of our nice hotel, with two nights of our holiday still to go.

'It's okay, Lolly,' said Dad, noticing my sad expression. 'There are loads of other places to stay. We'll go and find another room somewhere. Something cheaper. Let's wander around and see what we can see.'

But we didn't wander around, because leaning against their motorbike to the side of the hotel, waiting for us, were Ahmed and Siti.

She was in her school uniform, cradling her helmet and beaming.

'So, you had a real adventure?!' she said. 'Did you see any monkeys?'

'Lots. And a mouse deer!'

Her eyes widened.

'Really?'

'Really.'

I told her everything – about our dangerous journey, about hiding in the bush and all the things that we'd overheard Jennifer saying. I told her about my blog post, and what had just happened at the hotel. I tried to slow down, but my words tumbled out.

She seemed to understand most of it though. She smiled and gasped and groaned in all the right places.

Then I gave her a really puzzled look. 'But – what are you doing here?'

'My sister called to say that you'd been told to leave – the cleaners always know what is going on in a hotel. Do you have somewhere to stay?'

'Not yet.'

'Nawawi – the man over the road – he knows someone who has a hotel, not far from here. It is cheap. There is an empty room. We can take you there now. You are interested?'

I looked at Dad and he nodded – he was always interested in cheap things. And we definitely needed somewhere to sleep tonight.

But there was no way we could fit four people and our two big bags on that motorbike, even if Dad agreed to it (which was never going to happen).

Then . . .

*Ding!* The familiar tinkling of a bell.

We spun around. Our trishaw driver was waiting in his usual spot. Perfect.

Dad and I squeezed in with our bags and the driver turned to us. 'Same place?'

Dad shook his head. Ahmed and Siti had got on the motorbike by now and were ready to go.

'I've always wanted to say this,' Dad whispered to me. Then to the trishaw driver, he said, 'Follow that bike.'

And we did.

# 16  Going Nuts

The hotel was small, with three floors but no lift. Our tiny room had a fan instead of air-con, and two single beds with regular pillows and absolutely no chocolates.

But it was clean, the roof went all the way across and the people were friendly.

'You wanted somewhere real,' Dad said, as he sat down on his creaky bed, eyebrows up. 'This is okay though, isn't it?'

'It's great,' I said, and I meant it, though I secretly wished I'd stolen one of those amazing fluffy towels from our last place, and possibly a pillow too.

Dad took his phone out of his pocket, tapped the screen and then whooped with delight.

'What?' I said.

'Your blog is going nuts!'

'Going nuts?'

'*Thousands* of hits already – in just three hours! That's never happened to me. You're going viral, Lolly!'

'That sounds bad,' I said, because Ernest had a viral infection once and screamed his head off for a whole night.

'No – it's good – very good. It means that lots of people are reading it and passing it on to other people, who are passing it on to others, and so on. Which means that there'll be big pressure on the hotel people to leave Monkey Island alone.'

I grinned. So Jennifer might be wrong – things could change after all.

We called Mum and told her what we'd been up to (leaving out a couple of the more life-threatening moments, for now). We'd only been away for four days, but I was really missing her (and, surprisingly, missing Ernest and Oates too). I couldn't wait to see them all again.

I had a shower, which was small and less like a tropical

rainstorm, more like warm drizzle. Then we got changed into fresh clothes and, when the sun was setting (but still really hot), we walked over to Siti's restaurant – we'd been specially invited there by her mum.

There was a real party atmosphere at the restaurant. Most of Siti's family and a lot of the neighbours were there. Siti was serving, but she was able to take lots of breaks and chat to me. She was really happy. She'd just come from her extra English class and the teacher had been super-pleased with her. Plus, I think she was excited by the whole Monkey Island adventure.

Dad looked happy too. He and Ahmed talked about football for ages, using a combination of English and mime. And then Dad got up to have a chat with Siti's dad as he was cooking – with their neighbour Nawawi translating.

Her dad was cooking up a storm. He made *nasi lemak* – coconut rice (exotic food number four) and *beef rendang* (exotic food number five). Siti taught me word number five – *enak*, which means 'delicious'. I used it straight away with her dad.

And then, after we'd all eaten, Siti's mum went back to her house and came out with a plate of fruit.

It was durian. I was sure of it: I could tell by the smell from ten metres away.

It even *looked* horrible, like something Shrek might eat. She put the plate on the table in front of me, and Siti said, 'Try.'

It felt like everyone was watching me.

I scrunched up my face and popped the smallest

piece into my mouth. It was slimy, but I chewed it and swallowed.

It wasn't completely disgusting. But it wasn't great either.

'Do you like it?' asked Siti.

'Kind of,' I said, though my face must have told a different story, because everyone seemed to be laughing.

Dad was too, but then he smiled at me proudly, and I tingled with happiness: I'd now completed all the challenges. I couldn't wait to tell my class everything, and show them the videos.

And I still had one day of the holiday to go.

I looked at Dad. 'So, what's the plan for tomorrow?'

'Well,' he said, 'I had a word with Siti's dad – and he's so pleased with how much she's practising her English, and how happy she seems, that he's letting her have the day off school tomorrow – so you two can spend the day together. How does that sound?'

I whooped, because it sounded completely great.

Dad spent the last day of our holiday in the same food court where we'd had the coconuts. He was wearing his terrible shirt (Ahmed had unfortunately given it back to him last night). Dad sat at a small table, underneath a big fan, writing up the story of our adventure. They wanted to put it in the weekend magazine of the newspaper, not in the travel section, so it needed to be longer and – Dad said – funnier. So he wrote and wrote, drinking lots of milky iced tea and eating a lot. There were ten food stalls, and he was planning to sample something from all of them. I'd never seen him so happy.

I had a completely brilliant day too. It was the best one yet, in fact, because I didn't have to hide in any bushes, I didn't get in trouble for sneaking off, and I didn't once see Patrick (though I really wished I'd seen the look on his face the moment he realised that my blog had gone viral).

Siti and I had our own Adventure Club, just the two of us, roaming around. We had more fried bananas and some chocolate milk – in little clear plastic bags, tied up, with a straw poking out of the top. Then we went to the beach again to cool down in the sea, before she took me to a secret place – a place that no tourists knew about. She made me promise not to mention it in my blog.

There was a steep climb to get there – it was tiring and sweaty, but I was cured of my fear of heights now, and when we reached the top the view was completely spectacular. We sat on a rock, looked down at the sea for ages and talked. A lot. About our families, to begin with. It turns out that, wherever in the world you go, dads make terrible jokes, and mums are brilliant at working out when you're not telling the truth.

Then we talked about our schools – the kids at her

school seemed pretty much like the kids at mine – some were nice, some silly, some mean.

She asked me to show her some magic, so I did the disappearing coin trick – her mouth dropped open when the coin vanished, which meant that I must have been improving.

We talked about the adventure we'd had two days ago. She did an impression of me hopping on the hot sand, which was hilarious. So I did an impression of her yesterday when she'd thought she was in trouble with my dad. She laughed too.

And then we just sat there for ages, in the cooling breeze, looking out at the silvery blue sea – it was shiny and flat like polished metal. And at Monkey Island in the distance, green and beautiful and – I hoped – not about to change.

# One Month Later

*Hi Siti,*

*It's great to hear from you again. Congratulations on getting an A in your English exam! I got a B in my last English test – does that mean your English is better than mine, now?* 😊

*And I'm really happy that you're getting a bit more free time these days, at the beach and with your friend Damia. Say hello to the monkeys for me next time you see them: 'Oooh-ooh-aah-aah.' (That's monkey-ish for 'hi'.)*

*Things are going really well for me too. The best thing is, at school I'm not known as 'the girl who ran naked in a hotel' any more or even 'the kid who panicked at the climbing centre'. I'm 'the kid who helped save an island'! Emily Fellows is super-jealous, I can tell. Every time I smile at her she scowls. So I smile at her a lot.*

*Dad says that it wasn't only us that saved Monkey Island – he says that environmental groups and your local government were the ones that saved it in the end.*

But I think what we did – our two families – was really important too.

Mum says she's planning my next adventure, so that I can keep my blog going. I can't wait!

Write soon.

Your friend,

Holly

x

**Dave Lowe** grew up in Dudley in the West Midlands, and now lives in Brisbane, Australia, with his wife and two daughters. He spends his days writing books, drinking lots of tea, and treading on Lego that his daughters have left lying around. Dave's Stinky and Jinks books follow the adventures of a nine-year-old boy called Ben, and Stinky, Ben's genius pet hamster. (When Dave was younger, he had a pet hamster too. Unlike Stinky, however, Dave's hamster didn't often help him with his homework.) Find Dave online at @daveloweauthor or www.davelowebooks.com

Born in York in the late 1970s, **The Boy Fitz Hammond** now lives in Edinburgh with his wife and their two sons. A freelance illustrator for well over a decade, he loves to draw in a variety of styles, allowing him to work on a range of projects across all media. Find him online at www.nbillustration.co.uk/the-boy-fitz-hammond or on Twitter @tbfhDotCom

Have you read Holly's first two adventures?

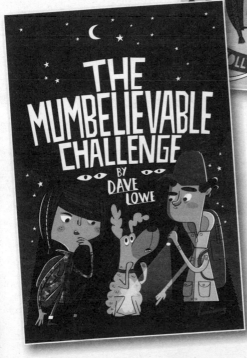

Available in paperback and ebook

# Piccadilly

## PRESS

Thank you for choosing a Piccadilly Press book.

If you would like to know more about our
authors, our books or if you'd just like to know
what we're up to, you can find us online.

## www.piccadillypress.co.uk

You can also find us on:

**We hope to see you soon!**